Nightwalker

BOOK ONE

Nightwalker
THE WARLOCKS OF TALVERDIN

K.V. Johansen

Library and Archives Canada Cataloguing in Publication

Johansen, K.V. (Krista V.), 1968-

Nightwalker / written by K.V. Johansen.

(The warlocks of Talverdin; bk. 1)

ISBN 10: 1-55143-481-4 / ISBN 13: 978-1-55143-481-0

I. Title. II. Series: Johansen, K.V. (Krista V.), 1968- Warlocks of
Talverdin; bk. 1.

PS8569.O2676N53 2007   jC813'.54   C2006-906509-8

Summary: In this otherworld fantasy, Maurey receives hints of his true ancestry
and must flee for the land of the Nightwalkers or burn in the philosopher's fire.

First published in the United States 2007
Library of Congress Control Number: 2006938696

Orca Book Publishers gratefully acknowledges the support for its publishing programs provided by the following agencies: the Government of Canada through the Book Publishing
Industry Development Program and the Canada Council for the Arts, and the Province
of British Columbia through the BC Arts Council and the Book Publishing Tax Credit.

Cover artwork by Yvan Meunier
Typesetting by Christine Toller

ORCA BOOK PUBLISHERS   ORCA BOOK PUBLISHERS
PO BOX 5626, STN. B   PO BOX 468
VICTORIA, BC CANADA   CUSTER, WA USA
V8R 6S4   98240-0468

www.orcabook.com
Printed and bound in Canada.

11 10 09 08 • 5 4 3 2

for my sister Sarah

CONTENTS

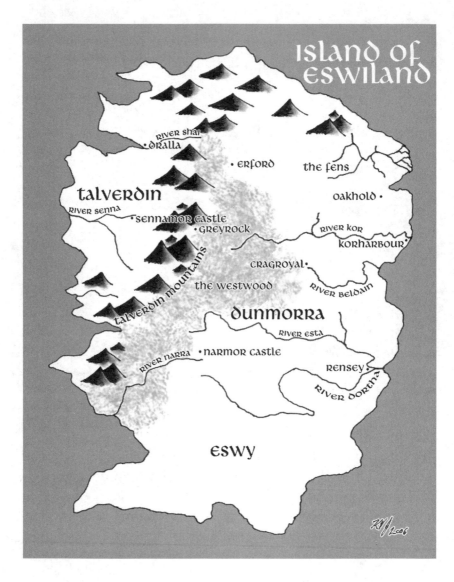

ISLAND OF ESWILAND

RIVER SHAI

•DRALLA

• ERFORD

the fens

talverdin

oakhold •

RIVER SENNA

•SENNAMOR CASTLE

RIVER KOR

•GREYROCK

KORHARBOUR•

CRAGROYAL•

RIVER BELDAIN

the westwood

dunmorra

talverdin mountains

RIVER ESTA

RIVER NARRA

•NARMOR CASTLE

RENSEY•

RIVER DORTHA

eswy

PART ONE

✣ CHAPTER ONE ✣
IN THE CELLARS

T he sing-song voice was getting closer.

"Hey, Warlock! Night-eyes! Nightwalker! Warlock, where are you? Night-eyes, come on out. Come on out, you grubby little slug."

I shoved myself farther back into the narrow gap between the wine barrels and the wall, clutching my mother's rings on their chain against my chest, praying to her shade to protect me. Calmic and his friends were going to find me this time, and the jeering would turn into shoving, the shoving into a beating as I tried to get away. It had happened before, when they caught me outside, taking a shortcut through the grammar school's enclosed yard on some errand or wistfully watching as the boys kicked a leather ball around the Fowler College green.

This time I had stood staring too long in the dining hall, where the masters of the college, the scholars and the grammar school boys all ate at the lengthy tables. I had been carrying bread to the lowest table where the schoolboys sat, when my eye was caught by the head table on its dais. There the Master of Fowler College, Arvol, ate with the other masters when they did not dine in their own households. On this occasion Master Arvol had not come alone. To his left sat his orphaned niece, the Baroness of Oakhold, the ward of his brother Holden, Chancellor of the University of Cragroyal, who was the king's chancellor, his chief minister, as well.

The young baroness lived in Chancellor Holden's grand house between the square of buildings that was Fowler College and the untidy cluster that was poorer Satman College. Although neither the grammar school nor the college admitted females, she spent a great deal of her time over in Fowler, nosing through our library or lurking in corridors and on stairways with her big black-and-white dog at her heels. She was trying, I guessed, to overhear the lectures, and I sympathized because I too hungered after learning and listened at doors to hear the masters instructing the scholars.

All the grammar-school pupils—the younger boys—and most of the older scholars were in love with the Baroness of Oakhold. I was a little in love with her myself. Who wouldn't be? She had elegant features—not soft and underdone, but not hard and mannish either—green eyes and long, red-gold curls that cascaded down her back from under her crisp lace caps.

I suppose it was more than a little in love. It took just a glimpse of her to make me forget whatever I was supposed to be doing and stand gawking, trying to think of some excuse to speak. I had said, "Excuse me, madam," once, when I was picking herbs in the garden and she was sitting in the shade of the pear tree, a book on her velvet-skirted lap. She had smiled at me a bit sadly as she moved to let me by. Those were the only words I had spoken to her. In the whole year she had lived at Cragroyal University, I don't think I had ever seen her looking happy. For me that was part of her mystery, part of her charm.

But staring at her there in the college dining hall: That was a mistake. She saw me and smiled wryly, raising her wineglass in a way that was almost a salute. A smile! I wrenched my gaze away, feeling the heat steal over my face and found big blond Calmic, the oldest boy still kept back in the grammar school, glowering at me from not two feet away.

I fled with my empty basket, but I knew I was in for it as soon as the meal was over.

I took as long as I could, scrubbing pots in the copper cauldron in the kitchen, but Calmic and his gang were waiting in the corridor beyond when Cook finally drove me out so he could lock the door—which he did to keep half-starved servants from getting into the larders and pantries, and scholars from stealing the pots and pans for their alchemical experiments.

"There he is!" Calmic's voice had rung out, and I had started running. "Filthy, spying freak, goggling at his betters, the little harlot's brat!"

I was taller than Calmic, but that wouldn't matter much. The six boys in his gang followed his lead in everything, and I was less than a servant—I didn't dare fight back. The only safety lay in not getting caught.

"You're gonna get it this time, Night-eyes!" he howled, and they pounded after me as I bolted for the great interconnected maze of vaulted cellars that ran under the seven colleges of the university and beneath the palace as well. I had good night vision and knew the lightless cellars better than any butler. Usually I could lose the boys there if I had a good head start, but this time Calmic and his gang were too close, and I darted into a dead-end wine cellar in my panic.

"Warlock! Night-eyes! Nightwalker!"

I hunched down behind the barrels. The voice was too close. There would be no escape for me this time. Maybe I'd be able to get in a few good kicks as they dragged me out. Maybe I'd be beaten by Cook, or by Master Arvol himself, when the boys were through. I certainly would be if I managed to injure one of them. I spoke a silent prayer to the shades of my mother and Dame Hermengilde, who had raised me. The dead were said to guard those whom they had loved in life. Through my threadbare smock and my too-large, hand-me-down shirt, I clutched the rings on their chain, rings my mother had worn when she died. They were all I had of her except my name. I pressed against the cold stone, trying to make myself nothing but a shadow, a darkness that the boys would not recognize.

The grayness came as it did sometimes—the world shifted all to gray, a thousand thousand shades as clear and detailed as if I saw by the light of the noon sun.

That grayness was something I never, ever, thought too much about, especially with cries of *warlock* and *Nightwalker* ringing in my ears.

Not even Calmic truly believed I was a warlock, a Nightwalker, one of that inhuman race of magicians who had inhabited the island of Eswiland before Good King Hallow came from the continent five centuries ago and drove them to the west, behind the impassable barrier of the Talverdin Mountains. I was only some dark-haired foreigner's bastard, but the names were a good insult and an easy way to hate me. Small-minded people always feel better with someone to hate. It covers up their secret fear that there is something to the world outside themselves.

I had my own fears, nothing to do with Calmic, but I kept them so tightly locked away that I was rarely aware of them myself. I was a foreigner's bastard. I had good night vision. That was all.

"Hey, warlock, come on out. We'll find you in the end, you know."

I braced my hands against the flagstone floor, ready to kick at the stomach of the first boy to squeeze in after me. I could hear them scuffling along, see the swirling shadows and yellow light of the candle they carried—except that it wasn't yellow. It was white, as all firelight was when the world turned gray on me.

I took a deep breath, my heart pounding.

Calmic stared down the narrow gap between the barrels and the wall. He looked right into my eyes. And then he went on through the archway into the next room of the wine cellar, the six boys pressed up behind him, keeping close to the candlelight. In Dunmorra and Eswy, the two human kingdoms of the island of Eswiland, we are taught very young to fear the dark.

The shadows came back once the boys were gone. I slumped down to the floor and shut my eyes, feeling weak, empty as an old sack. I could have sworn Calmic had stared right at me.

I didn't dare wait till the boys returned on their way out, though. The college butler would be coming down to lock up the wine cellars soon, and the boys knew it as well as I. They wouldn't waste much more time among the barrels.

I squirmed out, the gray fading to what I normally saw in the dark, a dim world of black shapes, deep, rich, velvet-shadow colors that glowed faintly with their own light, and occasional pearly glows. Other people didn't see this way. I had found that out when I was very small and had been warned by the people who had loved me never, ever to speak of it. My imagination, they had told me. I was merely pretending. They and I knew it was not true. I was not merely imagining, but I understood very young that I had to pretend even to myself that I *was* pretending, and never speak of it again. But my vision, better than an owl's, was what let me run at full speed through cellar passages and stairways lightless as a mine.

I headed for the door, intending to go along to the Old Stair, parts of which were older than the university or the palace itself. Spending the evening in the deeper cellars would keep me safe from Calmic until the boys' curfew.

Some of the lower cellars were empty abandoned places, where rats and strange spiders lived, but others were the crypts where the masters of the university were buried, their stone sarcophagi lying all but forgotten in lightless rooms. One of my favorite places was the Great Hall of the Kings, where all the past rulers of Dunmorra lay, each in a stone sarcophagus with his image carved atop it as if he were asleep in full armor. The boys rarely followed me in amongst the dead.

More passages stretched beyond and below the Great Hall of the Kings, but I had not explored even half of them, although I had once come out in the palace wine cellar. I hadn't lingered. An outraged butler's apprentice had chased me, waving a sampling glass and shouting "Thief! Help! Murder!" until I lost him in the vaulted tunnels and the dark.

One passage ended where it met an underground river, which flowed secretly beneath the city of Cragroyal. Icicles of stone hung from the roof, nearly touching the water. The water rolled silently in through a low-roofed tunnel, and out through another, broader and lower, where even in summer the rock overhead left only a hand span's space of air above the water. In the high waters of spring and fall, the river gnawed and fretted at the roof itself. I thought it must flow out to Cragfoot Lake. I had seen spotted lake-seals, little bigger than a cat, splashing about in it once and tried to follow them, crawling in the river's shallows like a seal myself, with the rock heavy over me and the river beneath. The tunnel opened out again after about a dozen yards and went on, the river beginning to chortle and splash. I had followed it until hunger warned me I would be late for my duties and I turned back with regret. I had never tried it again. It's not much fun getting cold and wet when you never have enough to eat and you get beaten for laziness when you huddle by the fire to dry the only suit of clothes you own.

I was just ducking out through the wine cellar door when I heard a shout from behind.

"There he goes, the little sneak!"

A light in the corridor had betrayed me—the college butler was coming down with a lantern and his keys. I ran away from the light, towards the Old Stair. There I hesitated. Up or down? There were voices above me, coming from the passage that connected to Chrysanthemum College; I bolted downwards, leaping the worn stone steps two at a time.

Behind me I heard booted feet and Calmic's voice whooping as if urging on hounds. Then an adult's voice, Butler's, bellowed, "You, boys! Stop right there!"

Safe, I was safe, I thought, pounding down past the archway to the Chrysanthemum College crypt and reaching the long spiralling stretch to the Hall of Kings. I grabbed the doorframe, spun through under the low arch and collided with a large bony body. We both smashed to the ground.

I scrambled up, babbling apologies and whirled around to flee again, but someone grabbed my shirt and yanked me back.

A hand thwacked against my head so hard my ears rang and my vision went red. I staggered and fell down again; this time I stayed there, crouched on the floor.

The man I had knocked over climbed slowly to his feet.

It was Chancellor Holden himself.

Of course it was, the back of my mind told me. Stupid boy. Today was the eleventh anniversary of the death of King Burrage. King Dugald would be burning offerings of bread and sweet oil to honor his father's shade and making libations of wine to the Lesser Power Fescor, guardian of souls, and the Great Power Geneh in her aspect as Queen of the Land of the Dead, and he would do it by his father's sarcophagus. Of course Chancellor Holden, his chief counsellor, would be with him. They said Dugald didn't sneeze without asking Holden's permission beforehand.

"Are you hurt, Holden?" asked a man at the back of the crowd of courtiers and men-at-arms.

"Only bruised, Your Grace," the chancellor said, continuing to brush dust off his elbows long after there was any need.

"Are you hurt, boy?" asked the same man.

I shook my head, trying to scrub the grime of the floor off my face with my sleeve, which probably wasn't much cleaner.

The man who had hit me—it was Master Arvol, the Chancellor's brother, but I did not see the Baroness of Oakhold anywhere, for which I thanked Sypat, Lesser Power of Chance—grabbed me by the collar and shook me so that the world spun.

"Are you deaf as well as clumsy, Night-eyes? Tell the king you apologize for interrupting his father's memorial prayers."

The king! I wiped my face again and tried to bow while kneeling on the floor. The king had spoken to me!

"The prayers were over, Master Arvol," King Dugald said, "and boys will be boys. Do you usually beat them for it?"

"A mild correction, Your Grace, only that. But this isn't one of the schoolboys. He's some harlot's orphan brat we keep on out of charity, though he's not worth his keep."

I was paid nothing—I might as well have been a slave. And it was Master Arvol who had stolen the money with which Dame Hermengilde had sent me to school. I didn't dare complain of that injustice to the king. The whole side of my head felt hot, and my ear rang so that everything sounded a little far away and watery. My eyes ran, but I stared anyway.

King Dugald was a young man with brown hair and blue eyes and a neat pointed beard. He wore a dark blue robe, the proper color for mourning rituals, open at the front, showing a very plain dark doublet and hose and a dark blue jerkin decorated only with jet beads and a bit of satin ribbon. He wore no crown at all. This was the first time I had ever seen him, though the palace and the university were so close together.

"Well, no need to beat him for that," the king said. "We can't help our parents."

I bowed again to thank him—not that what Master Arvol said about my mother was true. Then I tried to crawl away.

"Wait!" Chancellor Holden cried, and fast as a striking hawk he swooped forward and dragged me up by the front of my smock.

Even as he swooped, I realized that in the fall, my mother's rings had tumbled out of the neck of my shirt. I clutched at them but too late. Chancellor Holden jerked the heavy chain over my head and held it swinging before them all.

"A thief and a sneak!" exclaimed Master Arvol, sounding very pleased about it.

"I am not!" I yelled. "They're mine, from my mother. Give them to me!"

I grabbed at them, and the chancellor jerked them out of my reach.

The Master of Fowler slapped me again and knocked me to the floor so that I banged my head, and then things got confused. My nose was bleeding, and I was crying, "My mother gave them to Dame Hermengilde for me when she died, Your Grace. King Dugald, it's true. Make him give them back, please, Your Grace." And two of the king's men-at-arms in blue and black surcoats came at a nod from Dugald and politely pushed Master Arvol aside just as he was pulling back his foot to give me a kick.

But then Chancellor Holden was dangling the rings in front of the king, saying, "Your Grace, look. *Look!* After all this time, right under our noses."

And then the men-at-arms weren't defending me from Master Arvol anymore. They grabbed me up under the arms, and two more stood with their swords drawn.

⁜ CHAPTER TWO ⁜
WHEN I WAS BORN...

D
ame Hermengilde had told me the story of my birth, and if it sounded like a tale in a ballad, well, that did not make it any less true.

It was a night in late autumn, and the first storm of winter was howling over the forest, tearing off the last leaves and burying them in snow. Dame Hermengilde and her servants had just gone to their beds when a great baying arose among her hounds. Her steward went to the door, expecting to find some lost traveler or benighted pedlar who could be given a bench by the fire in the servants' hall for the night and sent on his way in the morning. Instead he found a woman, dressed in a ragged summer gown of light wool and a wrap that was little heavier. Her face was gaunt with hunger, her eyes, Harl Steward said, like two great dark pools in the light of his guttering candle, though better light showed them to be blue as the forget-me-nots that grow by the stream. She was soaked to the skin, for it had rained all that day before the night turned to snow, and her entire body shook with her shivering. She could not unlock her clenched and chattering jaw to speak.

Harl Steward set his candle aside and scooped the woman up as though she were his own daughter. He bellowed for his wife, Dame Hermengilde's housekeeper, and carried the woman to their own bed. Dame Hermengilde, Hanna Stewardswife and the maids stripped her, wrapped her in blankets warmed by the fire and forced hot broth between her lips.

The whole time, Dame Hermengilde told me, the woman stared at the ceiling, or through it, as if seeing something they could not.

She was expecting a child and shortly began to bring him into the world with never a cry or a scream, Hanna Stewardswife told me. It was as though she were already gone, safe from pain in some better place.

But she woke enough to the present world to tell Dame Hermengilde, in a voice like the whisper of a dying breeze, "His name is Maurey."

Dame Hermengilde, cradling the woman's head on her own arm, tipping the cup of broth to her lips with her own gnarled hand, asked, "My dear, what is *your* name?" The woman shook her head. She was as golden haired as the heroine in a ballad, and her dress said she was a lady, but her face was burned red and brown with the out-of-doors, like a hardy peasant wife's.

"No name," she said.

"But your family," Dame Hermengilde protested, "or the father. Someone should know. Someone must care."

"His father is dead," the woman said. "His family…is very far away. There is no one who will care for my Maurey."

And those were the last words she ever spoke, while I howled in the blankets beside her. *My Maurey.*

She died by the end of my first day of life. Dame Hermengilde buried her in her own family plot with a black stone that said only, *A lady, died in childbirth.* And little white roses twined over the stone.

I used to play there when I was a child.

One thing the women found when they washed her and dressed her in a clean white gown for her burial was that around her neck she wore a heavy golden chain, and on the chain two rings were strung. One was a simple silver ring engraved with daisies, the sort of ring a young girl might wear, not big enough for more than a grown woman's little finger. The other was a man's ring of thick gold with a square, dark red stone set in it. An oak leaf was carved into the stone.

They fed me on goat's milk, since none of the servants was nursing at that time, and I grew up in Dame Hermengilde's household. I was not quite servant, not quite grandson—it was a good and contented place. I knew my mother had been a lady. My father…well, he could have been anyone. A foreign sea captain or knight, a minstrel, an ambassador…anyone, so long as he was foreign, because on the island of Eswiland, especially in our northern kingdom of Dunmorra, the people were brown or red or blond of hair, and their eyes blue or hazel or gray…as mine were not.

No one would mistake me for a good Dunmorran like my golden-haired, blue-eyed mother. My eyes were black as night, my hair heavy, straight and raven black. Dame Hermengilde kept it cut evenly just below my ears, but I needed a trim twice as often as any of the men. Sometimes she would sigh theatrically, holding the shears. "It seems a shame to cut it. If only you were a girl, Maurey," she would say. "With a rope of such thick glossy hair hanging to your waist…Hanna and I would be beating the young men off from the door with brooms."

I doubt a girl as foreign-looking as I was would have fared any better than I did. Not that I had too bad a time of it then. Some of the children in the nearby village would run away when they saw me. "Nightwalker," they called me, as though I were one of the warlocks from the old tales and ballads, one of the inhuman race of magic-workers who had lived on the island of Eswiland before Good King Hallow came five hundred years before, to drive them into the west and make a human kingdom of this island.

Sometimes I would find a knotted cluster of holly and rowan twigs—supposedly a charm against witchcraft—thrown on the path where I was playing or dropped on our doorstep in the night. Dame Hermengilde laughed about such foolishness and taught me to laugh too. Everyone knew, she said, that in the southern kingdoms of the continent the people were darker than in the north or in Eswy and Dunmorra, the two human kingdoms of the island of Eswiland. She believed very hard in my foreign father and taught everyone else to believe it as well.

The flaw in her belief was that my skin was not black, or brown or even tanned. My skin was not even the roses and cream of a northern princess who has spent most of her life indoors. I never burned, never tanned. My skin remained milk-white even under the summer's sun. Hanna Stewardswife feared I was sickly and made sure I polished off my plate at every meal and never got my feet wet. Sickly, Dame Hermengilde's son hoped, and said aloud that I wouldn't live to adulthood. He resented the fact that his mother loved me. He never saw that he had killed her love for him himself by not loving her back. He never ceased to complain, whenever he did visit, about the folly of wasting money rearing a harlot's foreign brat.

And that was why, when she felt her own end approaching, the good Dame sent me away.

I was nine then, and Dame Hermengilde an old woman. I think she believed that her son would not use me kindly when he inherited her little manor. Not only was he jealous of his mother's obvious love for me, but he was the sort of person who hates foreigners merely because they are not like him.

Harl Steward took me south to the king's city of Cragroyal, riding on the old white mare. Like most small boys I looked forward more to adventure to come than back to what I was leaving behind, not understanding that you can never again have what is past. I did turn and wave, though, to the old woman propped on her two sticks standing at the garden gate with all the women of the household around her. Dame Hermengilde had wept enough for both of us when I kissed her farewell. They were all dear people and wished me nothing but good.

Dame Hermengilde had decided I was to be educated. She sent me to Cragroyal to be a pupil in the grammar school of Fowler College at the University of Cragroyal. After four or five years in the grammar school learning grammar and rhetoric, logic and arithmetic, studying history and poetry, I would move up to be a scholar of the college. I would study algebra and geometry and the secrets of the Great and Lesser Powers, learn to debate philosophy and law and the significance of the movements of the stars, and eventually take my degree. I would be a learned man: a lawyer or a physician, an astronomer or astrologer. I might even win a position as a master at Cragroyal University and spend my life studying and teaching. Dame Hermengilde was giving me a great opportunity, one that I now think she had secretly wanted for herself, but in those days young women were educated at home, if they were educated at all. Most were not, at least not in Dunmorra.

Dame Hermengilde also sent with me a small chest of money, which was to pay for my expenses until I took my degree. I would not be able to live the grand life as some of the pupils and scholars did, keeping horses and servants, passing their time in drinking and gambling rather than in study. But it would be enough—if the Master of Fowler College were an honest man.

Which he was not.

For two years I was a pupil in the grammar school. I excelled in all my classes, but I had no friends.

"Look at him," Calmic had said as I shyly took my seat among the boys in the dining hall on my first night. "Eyes like coal. Where're you from, Southie?"

I should have lied, claimed some home in the continental kingdoms or in the empire of Rona. I should have told them all I was a foreigner.

"Hermengilde's Manor, near Erford in the northwest," I said innocently.

Calmic snorted. "Not bloody likely. Talverdin, more like." He snickered, elbowed the boy beside him. "Look, they've sent a Nightwalker to school."

More snickers.

"Careful, Calmic. He'll put a curse on you."

"Going to ill-wish Calmic, warlock?"

"Hallow save us!" A boy clasped his hands in a mockery of prayer.

"Let him just try. My fists'll show him ill-wishing."

"Hey, Night-eyes! Ill-wish that!" A bun flipped across the table slapped into my stew, splashing me.

"Oooh. Get the warlock a bib."

And so it went, for two years. Then Master Arvol learned that Dame Hermengilde had died. He deduced, correctly, that her son was not likely to check on the foundling's education.

"Your tuition payment hasn't been sent this year," he told me, which was a lie. He had been given coin to last for the duration of my schooling. "You'll have to work for your keep now. That'll stop your troublemaking among the pupils, won't it, Night-eyes? Cook's expecting you down in the kitchen."

Through the years after that, I never heard my proper name on another person's lips. I was Night-eyes and fair game for anyone in a foul mood who wanted a cat to kick and couldn't find one. I'd almost forgotten myself that I had a name until I heard it again, whispered in a girl's soft voice, when I was locked in a dungeon cell under the palace.

But I am getting ahead of my story.

✳ CHAPTER THREE ✳
THE DUNGEON AND THE BARONESS

Every man in the Great Hall of the Kings was staring at me and at my mother's rings in the chancellor's hand. I felt as though even the stone effigies might sit up and point accusing fingers.

King Dugald took my rings from Chancellor Holden. His face paled and lost all its friendliness.

"They were my mother's, Your Grace," I pleaded. "I swear it. I swear it on her grave. I swear it by all-seeing Phaydos. Send to Erford and ask. Harl Steward, Hanna, they must still be there. They can tell you."

"Silence!" hissed the chancellor, and the word was so vicious that I obeyed, cowering on the floor.

"You recognize the woman's ring," the chancellor said to the king.

"Yes," King Dugald said, with a long look at me. "She'd had it since she was a little girl. It was a gift from her grandmother. She always wore it on that chain, for luck, she said."

"You know what the other one must be?"

The king frowned. "Some token of *his*."

"We know the false ambassadors brought something with them, something to still the enchantments to allow human passage to Talverdin. The king your father knew of it. He told me, though they had asked him not to speak of it. A ring, he said.

He was foolishly pleased that they trusted him, that they desired his friendship enough to consider allowing him to send envoys to their accursed magic-shrouded land." Holden lowered his head, eyes piously downcast, but I thought the purr in his voice sounded like a cat sitting amid a scatter of songbird's feathers. "He was too good a man for this world, too trusting, too easy prey for their lies and trickery. This oak leaf carved on the jewel is a sign of the house of the so-called royal warlocks. It is their treacherous king's own emblem. I will need to perform some tests, but I have little doubt. I can feel the power in it, even in your hand."

Chancellor Holden plucked the rings from the king and dropped the chain around his own scrawny neck.

King Dugald opened his mouth as if to protest, but the chancellor smiled reassuringly. "For safekeeping," he said. "A thing of power such as this can be very dangerous to those who do not understand it."

The king nodded, but his agreement looked reluctant. "What about the boy?" he asked.

"The creature," said the chancellor. "He must be tested by philosopher's fire, so that we can be certain of what he is. There is always a chance that he may be human, a legitimate son of your father."

"Nonsense," said Master Arvol. "You only have to look at him. I've always thought there was something unnatural about him, something evil. I don't know why I never realized before what it was."

"Nevertheless, we must not condemn him without proof," the chancellor said. His words seemed fair and just, but his smile was cruel. "Get torches. We'll keep him in the light until we find a secure place to hold him."

No one asked the king what he thought. A guard grabbed me under the arm and dragged me over to the wall, where the light of a boat-shaped oil lamp fell full on my face. He held me there, until other men-at-arms came back with flaming torches, which smelled of smoke and pitch and cast a restless pool of red light. Then we marched out of the Hall of Kings, with a guard at either side to support me. I was too sick and dizzy to stand on my own—sick with the bang on the head and with terror.

They took me through twisted passages and hallways, up and down stairs, until we came to the prison cells under the palace. There were not many prisoners. The palace dungeon was reserved for traitors and equally wicked men, not mere thieves and murderers. Furtive rats scurried from the light of the torches. The hinges of the first door were rusted so that it could not be moved, even with two burly men-at-arms heaving at it. But they soon found a cell door that would open, and the grim and silent warden who kept the keys.

King Dugald never left off staring at me.

Chancellor Holden smiled, fingering the rings that hung against his chest.

They weren't content with locking me in a cell. Master Arvol and the warden conferred, and the warden trudged off, returning with a sack of iron fetters.

"No," said the king.

"We can't leave him in the dark unsecured, Your Grace," the chancellor said. "My brother is quite right. He must be chained."

The king made no more protest. I watched dully as they locked heavy iron manacles around my legs, running the chains through a ring in the wall. They all filed out, and the warden closed the squealing door and locked it.

Then they were gone, their footsteps fading away, and I was alone.

Hours passed, and I stopped feeling quite so sick and dull-witted, though I still had a pounding headache. I tried to work my ankles out of the manacles but couldn't. I tried to pull the ring out of the wall, but that too failed. Not that either would have done me any good. It wasn't likely I could get out of the cell, even if I did get out of the chains. No matter what Chancellor Holden and Master Arvol thought.

Night-eyes. Warlock. *Nightwalker.*

I was not. I could not be.

My head ached, the front of my smock was all over blood from my nosebleed, and my mouth was horribly dry. There was a puddle on the stone floor. I cupped up some of the water in my hands. It tasted foul, but it was all there was.

Warlock. Nightwalker.

A Nightwalker would be able to use the darkness to step into the halfworld, to take himself out of the reach of human folk. When a guard looked in, he would see an empty cell, and the warlock could be away, out the open door, never seen. But even a Nightwalker wouldn't be going anywhere, chained to the wall.

Anyhow, I was no warlock. My mother had been a good human woman. Dame Hermengilde had said so.

In the past, the whole island of Eswiland had belonged to the Nightwalkers. They had traded a little with the humans on the continent, particularly the northern kingdoms, but, aside from that, humans and Nightwalkers had always left one another alone. Then King Hallow, who had been only a landless prince at that point, had assembled an army of mercenaries and sailed to Eswiland to make it a human land. Many battles had been fought, and many songs were still sung and stories told about Hallow the Conqueror, Hallow the Great. Not long after his death, the common folk of Eswiland had begun to count him among the Lesser Powers, invoking his protection against warlocks and ill-wishing.

The Nightwalkers were all warlocks, capable of dark magics. Their most fearsome skill was what had given them their human name, Nightwalkers. Not only was it said that they could see in the most lightless places, but that they could use darkness—night or mere deep shadow—to cross into the halfworld, where they could travel unseen by human eyes. But there were never very many of them, and the men of wisdom who came with King Hallow brought the philosopher's fire with them.

It took hard work and careful science to learn to make the cold white philosopher's fire, one of the secret arts that only a few were chosen to study, but it was a powerful weapon against Nightwalkers. It was said their bodies could not bear even the presence of it, although a human could walk through it unharmed. Philosopher's fire won the war for Hallow the Conqueror.

In the end, the Nightwalkers fled to the westernmost edge of the island, behind the Talverdin Mountains, and they made some last great spell so that no one could follow them. In the years that followed, princes and barons had led armies into the mountains. Sometimes they wandered in circles for months before finding their way out again. Sometimes whole companies marched over cliffs that they could not see. Sometimes there were avalanches. And sometimes the armies never came back at all. The Nightwalkers had gone on attacking humans for years, coming in small companies, wrapped in darkness, to burn castles and attack fortresses. And when they were captured, as sometimes happened, they were burned alive in the philosopher's fire.

In time, the descendants of Good King Hallow quarreled, and the human part of the island was divided into two kingdoms, Dunmorra to the north of the River Esta and Eswy to the south, and the Nightwalkers stopped raiding. They became almost a fairy tale, something to frighten bad children with. But people were still afraid of the dark because you never knew: A Nightwalker warlock might just step out of the shadows and cut your throat. Country folk still talked of seeing them slipping into forest shadow or riding by moonlight over the fields.

Then King Dugald's father, King Burrage, had decided to make peace with the Nightwalkers. Chancellor Holden had been furious. The Nightwalkers were pure evil, he said. They were the sworn enemies of humans and peace was impossible. To talk of peace was wickedness itself.

But King Burrage never listened to anyone once he had made up his mind. How he contacted them, no one then knew, but one day a party of Nightwalkers came to Cragroyal, riding their tall, moon-white horses. People still talked about that, the black-haired warlocks and their white horses and how they charmed the king and talked of peace and friendship.

They charmed the queen too. A prince of the Nightwalkers charmed her and bespelled her, and Queen Rhodora disappeared. Her maid said she had seen the beautiful queen in the garden on the back of a tall white horse with a Nightwalker holding the bridle. They had walked into the shadow between two yew trees, the maid said, and they had disappeared.

The rest of the Nightwalker delegation fled, either in guilt or fear. Perhaps they had not known what their prince intended. Perhaps they had.

King Burrage sent for Chancellor Holden. The chancellor did not say, "I told you so." He did not have to. The king sent out his knights, and the chancellor sent out university masters who had studied the arts of the Nightwalkers. They found the trail of the warlock prince and the queen. They hunted him and his captive, if she was his captive, through the length and breadth of Dunmorra. In the end Chancellor Holden captured the Nightwalker warlock, but the queen was never seen again.

The Nightwalker prince was burned to death in the palace square, burned in philosopher's fire. Minstrels made songs about heroic Chancellor Holden and the tragic abduction and death of Queen Rhodora.

Now those songs kept spinning around and around in my head, especially the verses about the execution of the Nightwalker.

I couldn't forget how Calmic had seemed to look right into my eyes in the wine cellar and had gone away without seeing me. How thin and insubstantial he had seemed, as though he were a ghost in another world—or as though I were.

I couldn't forget that I could see in the dark. I liked the darkness. It was safe. It was beautiful. At night, home at Dame Hermengilde's, the white roses glowed pearly silver, and the undersides of leaves flickering in the wind shimmered a soft gold. Water ran with streaks and swirls of moon-silver and moss-green.

Here in the lightless cell, the iron had an old rusty color, soft and dusty like a brown moth's wing, and even the foul puddle showed a faint, tired gray sheen.

That did not make me a Nightwalker.

Black hair, black eyes, white skin did not make me a Nightwalker. I was not evil. I was human.

Golden light began to leak through the tiny barred window in the door. At first I thought the guards were coming back to take me away to be tested by the philosopher's fire. I should have welcomed that. The white fire would not harm me. Of course it would not, could not, because I was human. But terror nearly overwhelmed me, so that all I could hear was my own heart beating. It took a moment for me to realize there was no chink and rattle of armor, just a soft rustling and a voice whispering urgently.

"Maurey?"

I barely recognized the word, so long had passed since anyone had addressed me by name.

"Maurey!"

"Who's there?" I asked.

"Annot."

"Who?" There were no Annots in the kitchen that I knew of.

There was a sigh. "Annot, Baroness of Oakhold."

"Oh. Oh!" I clambered to my feet and bowed. "Madam," I said.

"Are you *bowing*?" she asked.

"Yes, madam."

"Don't."

"Yes, madam."

"My name's Annot. You can call me that."

"Yes, m—Annot." For a moment, my heart was light. The Baroness of Oakhold had come to see me. She knew my name. Then my suspicion returned.

"What do you want?" I growled. "Did the chancellor send you?"

"His Honor, Cousin Holden? No." She snorted, a sound hard to reconcile with the serene sorrowful face that I had in my mind. "If he knew I was here, he'd have me beaten."

"He couldn't beat a baroness!"

"Hah! That's what you think. Maurey…"

"How do you know my name?" I interrupted.

"I've heard things," she said. "I asked a few of the masters."

"I'm surprised they remember," I said bitterly.

"Some of them do. Some of them say it's a shame. They say you were an outstanding pupil. They expected great things of you. Master Koffy, the astronomer, even said he thought you could have ended up chancellor of the university."

"He really said that?"

"I don't lie." Then she chuckled. "Not to you, I won't. To my dear cousins, I lie all the time."

"Madam—Annot, I mean. Why?"

"Because I hate them. Because they…"

I interrupted again. I had lost my manners through years as the dogsbody in the college kitchens. "Why'd you ask anyone about me?"

"Oh. Well, I saw you creeping around all the time and how everyone seemed to figure you were the one they were allowed to shout at and hit, and then someone mentioned you'd been a pupil, before. And I'd seen you watching me. You looked as alone as I felt. So I was curious. I thought—I thought you looked like an interesting person."

"Why didn't you talk to me then?"

She was silent a moment. "I was afraid of what would happen

to you if you were my friend. I'm supposed to make the king fall in love with me, you see. If *they* thought I had a friend they didn't approve of… There's nobody who cares about you. Nobody who would miss you."

"University masters don't run around murdering people like senators down in the Ronish Empire," I said.

"That shows what you know. Listen, Maurey, I don't have much time. *They* say you're a Nightwalker. Are you?"

"No! Of course not. You're as bad as Calmic, thinking just because someone has dark hair they have to be some sort of evil thing out of the west…"

"I don't think Nightwalkers are evil. All the stories about them…humans have done things just as bad, or worse, to Nightwalkers and to one another. Calling them evil is just an excuse to make old Hallow out a hero. He was nothing but a greedy vicious mercenary, coming to Eswiland, taking the Nightwalker's kingdom, just because he didn't want to be a poor landless knight. I *hate* that kind of greed. Stealing people's land just like Cousin Holden."

"Whose land did Holden steal?"

"Mine—or as good as stole."

I didn't point out that Oakhold and all the villages in her barony would once have been Nightwalker land, conquered by Good King Hallow and given to his followers.

"Anyway," the baroness went on without stopping for breath, "I think you are a Nightwalker. You really do look like one, the way the songs describe them, and you don't look like any Ronishman or any southerner that I've ever seen. Your skin's not dark enough. Do you know what those rings are that Cousin Holden took?"

"I didn't steal them. They were my rings!"

"I didn't say they weren't. But where did you get them?"

"They were my mother's. Dame Hermengilde—the lady who took in my mother and brought me up—she gave them to me and said they were all my mother had. And my mother wasn't a thief, so don't say she stole them."

"No. Your mother wasn't a thief. Maurey, do you know about the last queen, Dugald's mother, Queen Rhodora?"

"What about her? I've heard all the ballads. They all end with the warlock getting killed." For a moment, the panic I was trying to smother got loose, and my voice shook. But I was human. I had nothing to fear.

"Rhodora wasn't bespelled, you know. I've never believed that, and the country people sing ballads that say the same thing. Isn't that strange, when at the same time the Nightwalkers are the monsters hiding in every shadow in every tale they tell their children? Anyway, Rhodora's father made her marry King Burrage when she was younger than I am. They weren't in love or anything. Burrage was older than her father. Then when she had Dugald, they took him away from her and gave him to a nurse, so she didn't even get to look after her own baby. And then, when she was a grown woman, this handsome young Nightwalker came along… She fell in love with him, and they ran away together. That's what happened. Anyone can see that if they think about it."

"So? I've heard those ballads too. They end with the warlock getting burned anyway. And *she* goes mad with grief or guilt and drowns herself or wolves eat her or she dies in the snow in the forest as punishment, and Fescor refuses to escort her shade to Geneh. I don't see why it matters."

I was growing angry. I didn't want to see any point to what Annot was saying. I wanted her to be still a distant beautiful face

I could sigh over, not an insistent intense voice telling me things I didn't want to hear.

I wanted to be five years old again and home with Dame Hermengilde.

"They all came back to Cousin Holden's house after locking you up. I just sat in a corner pretending to read poetry, being sweet and quiet…I've gotten very good at sweet and quiet since I came to Cragroyal," she added, her voice bitter.

"Cousin Holden started marching up and down the room saying, 'After all this time, the Nightwalker brat and the ring, the talisman.'

"And Arvol said, 'But is it?'

"And Holden said, 'If you had my talent for the philosopher's arts, you wouldn't have to ask. I don't have to perform any rituals: I can feel magic seething in it. The spells held in this ring are so strong that it's a wonder mere stone and metal can hold them. Yes, Arvol, this is the talisman I've been looking for. With it, I can end the Nightwalker menace for good and all and make the lands of Talverdin Dunmorra's. Obviously the warlock let himself be captured so Rhodora could get away, and he gave the ring to her so she could win entry to Talverdin. But she chose not to go, or she was lost or some other fate overtook her, as was only just, for her sins.'

"And then Dugald said, 'You mean my mother is alive.'

"And Holden said, 'No, no, the treacherous woman—' and you know he was going to say something worse than 'woman' and just remembered in time that she was Dugald's mother, after all '—must have died or the ring would be back in Talverdin now, and her with it.'

"And the king said, 'I want my mother's ring, Holden.'

"And Cousin Holden took one of the rings off that chain and gave it to him. But Holden kept the other one tight in his hand as if he were afraid the king might steal it. Then they realized I was there, and Cousin Arvol sent me away. I listened at the door…"

"But that's my mother's ring!" I cried, outraged. "He can't give it to the king. He doesn't have any right!"

I was so busy denying half of what she said that I was ignoring what the rest of it meant.

The Baroness of Oakhold sighed. "Maurey?"

"What?"

"It's your mother's ring."

"That's what I said."

"It's Dugald's mother's ring too."

"No."

"Yes."

"That isn't true. None of it's true."

"So what, then? Your mother met Queen Rhodora in the forest and took her ring?"

"Maybe. Maybe she helped the queen, and the queen gave her a ring to thank her…"

"And she just happened to have a Nightwalker lover herself and had a Nightwalker baby. Of course."

"But…"

"Maurey, Queen Rhodora was your mother. King Dugald is your brother. Your half-brother, really."

"No!"

"And you are a warlock."

"But…"

"I thought you should know. Since they're going to torture you for it anyway."

"But…"

"I've tried to find the keys, but the warden has them," she said. "They're planning to test you with the philosopher's fire, because if you aren't a warlock, then Queen Rhodora was already pregnant when she ran away, and you're King Burrage's legitimate son and a full human. But they don't believe that and neither do I. Maurey, if you can do any warlock magic, you'd better do it and get out of here. If you can go into the halfworld…"

"I can't!" I yelled. "I'm not a Nightwalker! Go away and leave me alone! If they think sending you down here will make me say I am, they're even stupider than you. Just go away!"

The candlelight whirled and vanished, and with a sound like a sob the Baroness of Oakhold was gone.

✳ CHAPTER FOUR ✳
THE BARONESS AND SOME PIGS

To my shame, after the baroness left me I huddled into my corner and wept like a child. I was furious that the chancellor and Master Arvol had sent her down to taunt me. And I was furious at myself for yelling at her and being so rude when I knew in my secret heart that no one had sent her, that she had come because, as she had more or less admitted, she saw something likeable in me. And most of all I was furious because everything she said was true.

Of course I knew what I was. When I had begun to suspect, I couldn't have said. After I came to Fowler College, at any rate. It's easy to tell yourself lies, to ignore, to explain away all the little signs of something. I have seen people do it with the symptoms of some grave illness. They refuse to acknowledge, not only to their friends or their physicians but to themselves, what they wake in the night knowing is the truth—that they are dying.

Or that they have Nightwalker blood.

Of course I had known.

But what I had never thought about, never suspected, was my mother's name.

Rhodora. The lost queen. Her Nightwalker prince had let himself be captured to save her, to buy her time to get away. And they had killed him. My father. Chancellor Holden had

killed my father, and once he had proved to the king that I
was…what I did know I was, he would kill me.

I was sick with terror. I wrenched at my chains and dragged
at the ring in the wall with the full force of my body. I tried again
to scrape the manacles off over my heels, but it was impossible.
Still sobbing, I fought against the iron like a wild animal, like a
creature driven mad, ripping at my own body without noticing the
pain. Finally, though, the throbbing in my hands and the searing
agony of my feet became too much to ignore. My ankles were torn
and bleeding, swelling up around the tight bands, and my fingers
were blistered and bleeding too. I could not get free.

I curled up there against the wall, shivering with cold and a
sort of aching that was more in my soul than my body. I was used
to being alone, but never in my life before or since have I felt so
entirely desolate as I did that night.

I did not sleep. When I could not cry any longer, I simply
sat, stunned and still as a fox in a trap.

Guards came for me in the morning, not that there was any
window in this deep cellar to show that morning had come. The
red torchlight flooded in, and the door squealed open, and two
men-at-arms unfastened the fetters on my legs, while two more
held the light close.

"Poor lad needs a physician," one of them grunted.

"None of that," said the other. "His kind don't deserve sympathy. You're letting his enchantments get to you."

If only I had known any enchantments to get at them with.

I walked numbly between the guards, up stairs I didn't know,
to the Hall of Judgement in the palace. Servants clustered in
corners, watching, whispering. Many of the masters of Fowler

College were there in their black gowns and bright hoods. Some looked sorry, but most of them gawked, fascinated, as though I were some sort of show.

I was marched up the length of the long room to the king's throne of judgement. Chancellor Holden stood behind a square table at Dugald's side, dressed in his finest black silk gown, the purple and white hood of Rensey, the Eswyn university where he had studied, as carefully arranged as a lady's dress to show off its stripes of color to best advantage. His hands were clasped together inside his sleeves, and he kept rising and falling on his toes as if he could barely contain an urge to bounce up and down in his excitement. Master Arvol hovered at his side.

Lamps stood in niches all along the walls. Candles in tall candelabra flanked the aisle and the throne, and more burned in glittering golden chandeliers. They left no chance of a shadow through which I might enter the halfworld, not that I had the faintest idea how to do such a thing. If I had done so before—and it seemed likely I had, there in the wine cellar—it had been by accident.

"Your Grace," Chancellor Holden said with a quick bow to the king, "my friends. We are here to test the boy called Maurey, a servant at Fowler College, to determine if he carries the curse of Nightwalker blood. I call on the Seven Powers and especially Phaydos, may he bring us the light of truth, and Mayn, may her wisdom guide us, and Geneh, who holds the balance of life and death. I ask all you gathered here to witness this testing, so that none may say we acted unjustly."

That formality out of the way, he gave me a hungry, sneering sort of smile and turned his attention to the table before him.

The king, very grand in robes of crimson velvet and cloth of gold, was watching me. I glared at him, and he shifted uncomfortably on his throne, looking away.

Chancellor Holden took a wooden cup of white chalk dust and, moving with great care, sprinkled out a circle around a broad silver bowl set in the middle of the table. He drew a second circle of red dust and a third of black. Then he poured various odd glittery liquids out of dark glass flasks into the bowl. He added other powders and stirred the mixture with a wooden stick.

The making of the philosopher's fire was a difficult and dangerous art. The ingredients were hard to come by, and, supposedly, if the incantation was not properly pronounced, the man summoning the fire could die.

I prayed to the shades of my mother and Dame Hermengilde for protection, prayed to the Lesser Power Sypat, who ruled fortune and chance, for something to go wrong, but Chancellor Holden was an expert in the secret arts of the philosophers.

Some scholars muttered that these arts were no different from magic and just as wicked. Others said that they had been learned through long study of the nature of the world and so were the greatest science a human could achieve—not like Nightwalker magic, which was of course evil, since it was Nightwalkers doing it.

Nothing went wrong. Chancellor Holden extended his hands over the bowl and began to murmur quietly in one of the dead languages of the continent, Ancient Ronish, which nobody actually spoke any more, even in the Empire of Rona.

The bowl began to emit a soft silver light.

It would not hurt me. My mother was human. I had to prove to them that it did not hurt me.

The glow erupted suddenly into a great pillar of white flame, snapping and crackling as it burned the air, twining around Chancellor Holden's hands. The onlookers gasped. No doubt few of them had ever seen the philosopher's fire before, unless they had been present at the Nightwalker prince's—my father's—execution.

I didn't even know his name. In the ballads he was just "The Warlock Prince, the jet-eyed one."

He was suddenly a very real person to me. He had stood, as I did now, watching the chancellor prepare the fire, watching the white flames snap and roar. And he had known what was to come. But his had been a much greater fire. They were only testing me. Only testing. And my mother was human. That had to count for something.

The flames steadied to a slow graceful wavering. They seemed to hum a single sweet note, just on the edge of hearing.

"Bring the boy forward," the chancellor ordered.

I clenched my teeth. Now, when there were people to see, I was not going to cry or scream. I would show them. I walked forward between the two guards, staring the chancellor straight in the eye.

The note the white flames sang changed. It grew harsh and hissing, and the flames began to leap wildly again, snapping and cracking as though they burned pitch-filled pinewood. They reached towards me as if driven by a strong wind.

I felt as though my skin were on fire. I knew I must plunge my hand into the bowl of white flames. I must, to prove to them that I was human. I took another step, and one more, but the very air burned. I could not breathe. I could not see. I could not feel the floor under my feet. Everything had become a hot roaring whiteness. Far, far away, I could hear Master Arvol shouting, "Behold! The Nightwalker cannot even *approach* the flame!"

And someone else yelled, "Enough! Holden, that's enough! You're killing him. Stop!"

But the pain grew worse and worse, until I could hear nothing but a shrill screaming sound, and all I wanted was to be dead, so there would be no pain.

Then it was gone. I was lying on the floor, curled into a trembling ball. The screaming had been me. But I was not burned; the philosopher's fire had not touched me.

Not yet.

A guard pulled me to my feet. I swayed and sagged in the man's grasp and then was allowed to collapse back to the floor again.

"It would take more than the mere presence of the fire to kill a Nightwalker, Your Grace," the chancellor was saying to the king. "But never fear, a greater fire will cleanse us of his evil."

"I don't want the boy killed."

"Will you allow the evil of the Nightwalkers to spread over the land once again, Your Grace? If you allow this one to live, what of the next warlock who is captured, and the next? If they lose their fear of us through your weakness, what will stop them prowling the land at will, killing as they please?"

The king bit his lip and said nothing.

"I will make the arrangements," Chancellor Holden said. "It must be soon."

"No. I will not have him killed. *He is my brother.*"

An excited hiss ran through the hall. The masters must not have known that part of it. No one need ever have known, but the king cried it aloud. I forced my eyes open, tried to get up on my knees, thinking that if I begged, pleaded, promised to go into exile, perhaps Dugald would spare me. My throat failed me, though, and I could only gasp raggedly, wordless. The look the chancellor gave Dugald was the sort someone gives you before they beat you. The king was a grown man, but he quailed and scowled like a powerless little boy, frightened and defiant and surly in one, as though the throne he sat on counted for nothing.

Chancellor Holden glowered out over the hall, and everyone fell silent again.

"He may be what you say, Your Grace, to your late mother's shame. But that does not alter what he is. I quite understand how you might be moved—he looks so harmless, huddled there. But the wolf pup grows to be a killer of sheep and men, and never forget..."

A great baying drowned him out, as if the wolf the chancellor spoke of was hunting in the palace. And another sound, high-pitched, excited—squealing.

The masters began to murmur and look around, no longer paying the chancellor any attention. Even the guards were distracted, looking towards the doors. Only the king never moved, staring at me with a mixture of anger and misery.

The great doors burst open, and a sea of moving color flooded into the Hall of Judgement, squealing and grunting.

Pigs. White pigs, black pigs, red pigs, spotted pigs. They thundered up the aisle as if all the demons of Talverdin were after them. Behind them was a dog, an enormous, long-haired, black-and-white beast of the sort that shepherds keep to guard their herds from wolves in the northern mountains. I knew that dog. It was the Baroness of Oakhold's faithful shadow. And with the dog, driving on the swine with shrill yelps and a waving stick, a pack like a pedlar's on her back, was the baroness.

These were not cute little piglets. They were full-grown sows and a couple of boars from the royal sties. They were huge. Each weighed three or four times as much as a grown man. Frightened and angry, they were all tusks and flint-sharp hooves.

I scrambled to my feet just as the tide of pigs reached me. One of the men-at-arms fell, screaming, wrapping his arms around his head to protect himself. The chancellor and Master Arvol climbed onto the table, scattering the flasks of rare and no doubt expensive alchemical ingredients. The guards clustered around the king, who jumped up to stand on his throne, the trailing train of his topmost robe looped up over his arm. A candelabrum went over, the carpet began to burn, and a shower of blue sparks rose like a fountain as one of the chancellor's alchemical ingredients caught fire. Pigs squealed and milled around, bunching away from the smouldering wool.

"Fire!" shouted the king, almost happily, it seemed to me, as the orange flames licked up, and then the masters panicked, rushing out of the hall just as a swarm of servants came rushing in to see what all the noise was. The two crowds met and tangled at the door, neither able to fight through, everyone shouting at the top of their lungs.

The men-at-arms, dragging their injured fellow, were trying to beat a path through the pigs to lead the king to safety. The last I saw of Dugald was a grinning face looking back over his shoulder, before the guards hustled him out a side door hidden in the panelling.

"Come on, quick!" And there was the Baroness of Oakhold, grinning as broadly as the king. She grabbed me by the hand and whistled sharply. The dog bounded to join us, silent now. The sounds of the pigs grew fainter as the beasts found their way back out the doors to freedom.

"Stop them! The Nightwalker!" the chancellor bellowed, but

no one obeyed. He and his brother were trapped on the table, the carpet around them ablaze. Servants and masters were running with pails of water to quench the flames. "Annot, you little harlot, your soul will be damned to the outer darkness for this!"

Annot, running and towing me along, came to a sudden stumbling halt. She whirled around and screamed out over all the noise, the crackle of flames and the shouting: "So will yours be, for my mother's murder!"

Then she turned again and ran, shoving me through the door by which the guards had left with the king.

We found ourselves in a narrow corridor, lit by small windows high overhead.

"Right, turn right," the baroness said, pushing at me as I stumbled. It took all my strength and will just to stand upright. "You can apologize for yesterday later."

I didn't answer. The baroness jerked me to a halt, squeezed past, and thrust her full weight against a door I had not even seen.

They were still shouting in the Hall of Judgement, but from the sound of it, the fire was under control. I could make out Chancellor Holden's voice calling, "They're in the back passage, you fools. This way!"

"Help me!" the baroness ordered, and I added my weight to hers. Feet pounded down the corridor, guards and servants and the chancellor. But the door gave way, and we tumbled through onto a narrow descending staircase.

We ran, the dog bounding ahead, Annot half-dragging me. The wooden stairs ended on a stone landing. Spiralling stone steps continued down. The sounds of pursuit slowed.

"This is supposed to go into the cellars," she panted. "But I didn't have time to check whether it really does or not. Pray Sypat it does. Maurey? Maurey, pay attention." She shook me. "I'm sorry. You looked horrible up there, and I'm sure you're awfully sick, but you have to lead the way now. I don't know the cellars and I can't see a thing."

That was when I realized we had run down out of the reach of even the faintest light from the back passage windows. The stone, a soft, bluish color, was giving me what light it could. Annot's hair gleamed like true gold.

Above, Chancellor Holden's voice bellowed for candles.

I took Annot's hand again and started downwards. The dog pressed close against her side.

✤ Chapter Five ✤
The Hidden River

"Which way now?" the Baroness asked.

We stood in a tall archway, a landing on the Old Stair. Annot was blind, knowing only what was under her feet, but to me the stones here, different from those higher in the castle, had a dim pearly sheen, barely visible even to my eyes.

"I don't know." The words came from my throat hoarse and scraping. "Where are we going?"

"Out! Are you all right? Was it very bad?"

"Yes."

Her grip on my hand tightened. "I thought they'd killed you already, when I saw you lying there on the floor. Maurey, I'm so sorry. It took longer than I thought to get the pigs through the palace courtyards. They don't herd as well as sheep."

We had lost the men who followed. Somewhere in the labyrinth of stairs and vaulted passages the chancellor had taken a wrong turn. But that wouldn't stop our pursuers for long.

"Is there a way out through the cellars that doesn't take us up into the colleges?" asked Annot. "Because they'll be expecting us to try to escape that way. And anyway, there are only the four gates out of the university campus. They'll be watched. But I've heard that the tunnels down here go on for miles."

"Maybe," I said. "I've never come across any way out, other than into the colleges or the palace. Madam..."

"Annot."

"Annot, I'm sorry."

"Oh," she said, "my apology. Thank you." She shrugged. "You were scared. Angry. Not at your best. I understand. I forgive you." She smiled faintly.

"Yes," I said, "but still, I was pretty nasty. I mean..."

"It's all right." She squeezed my hand. "Just you wait till I lose *my* temper. So what do we do now, if there isn't a way out? Hide until they stop looking for us? That could take a while. Maybe we could climb over the campus wall somewhere, if we could sneak out through one of the colleges at night."

"Where are we going?" I asked. "Are we going to live in the forest like outlaws, poaching deer?"

"Probably," she said, with a grin. "I want to go home, back to Oakhold. But I can't. That's the first place my dear cousins will look. I have some other cousins down in Eswy. They're nice people—for Eswyn pudding-boilers." She laughed at the old joke about Eswyn cookery. "No, my cousins are very kind good people, and their cook makes the finest suet pudding you could ever hope to eat. But the Eswyn are even more afraid of warlocks than we Dunmorrans are. So what I thought..." She took a deep breath. "I thought we could go to Talverdin."

"To Talverdin!" I repeated. "Nobody goes to Talverdin. The mountains are enchanted. Whole armies have been lost for years just trying to retreat out of them. And anyway, the Nightwalkers..."

"Yes?" she asked sweetly.

I shrugged and remembered that she was blind here. "They won't like me any better than humans do," I muttered.

"I don't know about that," she said. "I've studied a lot of

history. Of course, half the time it's people like Cousin Holden writing it, so it's hard to know what to trust. But it seems to me that the Nightwalkers weren't nearly so bad as the humans during the wars. I mean, most of the worst things that were done were done by us. People say the Nightwalkers killed whole villages, but when you look at what people wrote, people who were actually there—no one writing at the time said that. The warlocks weren't the ones executing children by burning them to death in philosopher's fire. If you read what the chroniclers wrote back then and pay attention to what they say and what they don't say, you realize the Nightwalkers were the ones with all the virtues that the knights were supposed to have. *They* were honorable. *They* kept their word. *They* didn't torture people for the fun of it. *They* didn't kill enemies who yielded. *They*..."

"All right," I said.

"And how'd you feel if someone came and said that just because you weren't human, they could take your kingdom away? No wonder they fought."

Well, if I was going to admit to myself I was a Nightwalker, I might as well do so aloud, and if I was a Nightwalker, then... "What do you mean, if?" I snapped. "If I'm a Nightwalker, then someone *did*."

But she only chuckled. "Well, you're as much human as you are Nightwalker. It's silly to say you aren't."

I sighed. Suddenly all the terror and pain seemed to catch up with me. My entire body felt like one huge throbbing bruise, yet I could have fallen asleep just leaning against the wall.

"I guess you're right. So what are we doing?"

Annot seemed to understand. Talverdin was too far away to think about right now.

"We either have to find a way out of here or find a place to hide until they think we must have already escaped and stop searching. You can't do that going into the halfworld thing, can you?"

"I don't know," I said. "Not on purpose."

The dog turned and looked back up the stairs, its lip curling into a silent snarl.

"Someone's coming," I said.

"Which way?"

I started downwards. There wasn't that much below us now, only abandoned crypts so old no one remembered who lay in the stone tombs. There was even one crypt—I had found it once and never could find it again—where the uncoffined bodies had been stacked in niches in the walls, one on top of another, victims, perhaps, of some plague. The skeletons had long ago settled into jumbled heaps of bones. I had some vague idea of hiding there, if I could find the place. The chancellor probably didn't know it existed. Then I had a better idea.

"The river." I whispered, because I was catching faint noises, distant voices above. They must be searching methodically, level by level. "We can hide there. Maybe even get out that way."

The dog growled.

"Quiet, Blaze," Annot ordered. "And stay close, boy."

It took me a moment to realize she had meant the dog. I would have to get used to having a name again.

We didn't run anymore. I couldn't. At first I led, but Annot finally had to let go my hand and slide her arm around my waist to support me.

I didn't hurt too much to appreciate that. In fact, I was so distracted with wondering if I dared put my arm around her too, and what she would do if I did, and would she think it just faintness, and if she did, was that fair, that I nearly missed the way.

That reminded me how close danger was on our heels. Death, for both of us. They beheaded traitors, and stealing a proven Nightwalker from under the nose of the King of Dunmorra and the Chancellor of Cragroyal University was probably treason, even for a baroness. Especially for a baroness. My life was not the only one at stake.

A low archway opened off to a brick-walled passage. The brick, ancient and crumbling, was an earthy red, soft, warm and, somehow, safe. Brick gave way to a roughly carved tunnel like a mine, which took frequent jagged turns. Here the rock looked, to me, a soft cream color, streaked with brown and amber and faint shadows like clamshells, although I had brought a candle down once and found it to be actually a dull gray.

"Where are we now?" Annot asked.

"Almost to the river." Even as I spoke, the tunnel ended. We stepped out into a vast echoing cavern, as big as the Hall of Judgement. Steeples of stone rose from the floor, and others dripped from the ceiling, glistening with damp. Sometimes they met, making pillars that added to the illusion that we had entered some underground hall, the sort of place the beautiful witch-trolls were supposed to live in, if you believed the Gehtaland ballad singer I once heard perform for the masters as they dined. The cavern echoed to the gentle sound of water. Perhaps the entire cave had been gnawed out by the river long ago, but now the river lapped gently at its stone shore on the far side of the cavern, entering from who-knew-what mysterious underground realm, passing out to flow through more lightless channels until it found the open sky—I hoped.

"I can smell the river," Annot whispered, and the last word echoed around us…*ver, verr, errr.* "I'm awfully thirsty, Maurey. Do you suppose it's safe to drink?"

Blaze, who must have been as blind as Annot in that dark place, sniffed, splashed into the shallows and lapped eagerly.

"I guess so. Here." I led her across the cavern's uneven floor, until she stood at the water's edge. "Don't fall in. It's right in front of you."

She laid down the stick she still carried and felt her way forward until her hand found the river. She cupped up water in both hands, and I did the same, watching the shimmer of colors on the water's surface, clear and soft as twilight, not like the puddle on the floor of the cell. That was the last time I had drunk. Small wonder my tongue felt as though it were carved from splintery wood.

The water was winter-cold and started me shivering when it hit my stomach. I held my hands in it, watching the river wash away the dirt and dried blood from my torn fingers. Next, clenching my teeth, I plunged my feet in, hissing with the pain.

"Cold water's not good for open wounds," Annot said, guessing what I was doing from the sounds.

"Neither's dirt, Dame Hermengilde always said."

"I suppose. I brought some goosegrass and primrose salve I used to use on my horses. I thought you might need it. But we can't stop here, can we?"

I sighed. I wanted nothing more than to lie down and sleep. "No, that tunnel's not used much, but they'll come down here eventually. I thought we could go down the river a ways."

"Where does it come out?"

"Cragfoot Lake. Maybe. I've seen lake-seals in here, anyhow, and they must have come up from the lake."

"It's worth a try," Annot conceded. "At least it'll be a place to hide for a while."

"You're going to have to get wet," I warned. "The rock comes right down to the water, and we have to go under."

"For how far?" she asked. "I can hold my breath, but Blaze can't."

"Not very far." I studied the place where the river left the cave, a low hole in the wall. The water had been lower when I had tried to follow the river's tunnel downstream. But we had no choice. Drowning was better than burning, anyway. "There's a little space between the water and the roof of the tunnel. Maybe if we go one on each side of the dog, we can get him through."

In the end, to stop Blaze thinking he was abandoned and beginning to howl, I went through first, carrying Annot's pack, her stick, which turned out to be a bow, and the quiver of arrows that hung from her belt. The pack was very heavy. I wondered aloud if she'd stolen the chancellor's silver, and she grinned.

"I just took anything I thought would be useful."

The pack was made of oiled canvas—not really waterproof, but everything was well-wrapped, she said, and if I went quickly it shouldn't get too wet. But if I got her bow soaked...

I scraped my knuckles badly, holding it and the quiver above the water. But my hands were so torn up already it didn't really matter.

Blaze was much harder to manage. We tried to coax him to lie down with us and crawl in the water, but he ran up and down the river's edge instead, whining. Finally Annot took him by the collar and led him out into deeper water. I was worried by that, because if she slipped, wearing those heavy woollen skirts, she would be pulled down and dragged away by the current.

We managed it. Once the water was up to his back the big dog didn't have much choice other than to swim, and we were able to pull him under the low rock roof, his skull scraping along it. I was glad Annot couldn't see him, though. I've never seen an animal's eyes hold such terror.

But we made it through to where the tunnel widened again, so that the river had a steeply sloping shore of rock to either side of its channel. The roof rose again as well, giving us room to stand upright. Annot and I helped one another to climb out, water pouring from our clothes. Blaze shook himself violently and capered about, letting out a couple of deep barks of joy before Annot managed to silence him.

Then, dripping, we went on, Annot carrying the pack again, with her bow resting on her shoulder.

Maybe she really did plan to live like a forest outlaw. There were probably worse lives, now that I came to think of it. We could be like Jock Wildwood and his Fuallin-month Queen, gather a band of faithful followers, rob the rich…I realized I was walking in a sort of waking dream, smelling rotten leaves and spring flowers, hearing the wind in the branches, seeing the gray trunks of the great oaks and pines.

"We have to rest," Annot said, waking me, and I realized she was half carrying me. "I don't think I can walk much farther. These wet skirts are just too heavy. Is it safe to stop yet?"

She did not mention the pack or how heavy I must have been, leaning on her.

I had no idea how far we had walked. I rubbed my eyes and looked back. The narrow tunnel of the river curved away around a bend. The tunnel roof looked as though it had been melted at some point, and dripped down, reaching for the water.

"Yes," I said, simply, and sat down where I stood.

"You need to eat," Annot said, struggling out of the straps of the pack. "If the oatcakes are wet, we can call them cold porridge. And you were bleeding, back there in the Hall of Judgement. I want to bandage you up."

But I sank into sleep so swiftly that Annot's voice, wondering if it was safe to light a candle, and if her tinderbox would still be dry, seemed only part of some troubling dream.

❈ CHAPTER SIX ❈
CRAGFOOT LAKE

When I awoke, it was to what seemed a brilliant blaze of golden light. In fact it was only the smallest of flames, a beeswax candle in a horn-sided lantern.

"Have you ever tried to light a candle from a tinderbox?" Annot asked.

"No," I said, blankly.

"Well, the sooner you learn some useful warlock magic, the better," she said. "I'm sure warlocks don't have to mess around with flint and steel. It took me ages to get a spark into the tinder, and then trying to get the wick to light, before all my tinder was burned up..."

"If someone sees the light..." I began.

"They won't. The water was nearly up to the roof where the river left the cave, remember, and we went around a bit of a bend too. Are you feeling better? You've been sleeping for hours. At least, I think it must have been hours. I fell asleep myself, for a bit."

The baroness was laying food out neatly on a napkin as she spoke, oatcakes and dried apple slices and crumbly cheese, so sharp and tangy I could smell it. My mouth started watering.

"Eat," she ordered. "You're thin as a wraith. I'm surprised I can't see right through you."

I didn't need any second urging.

My torn wrists and ankles had been bandaged up with strips

of white linen. I assumed Annot had torn them from her petticoat. That was what ladies did in ballads, bandaged up their knights with their petticoats. It was the main reason for wearing them, as far as I could tell.

While I ate, washing down the dry oatcakes with handfuls of river water, I studied Annot. She was not much like the picture of the Baroness of Oakhold I carried in my mind, a girl shy and delicate, ethereal as a pining ballad maiden. No longer dressed in velvet and lace and ribbons, she wore sturdy green wool. Her skirt and petticoats were the divided sort ladies wore for riding if they did not use a sidesaddle, slit at the front and back so they could ride astride, but so full a gentleman would hardly notice she wore pantaloons of the same cloth as the skirt beneath, and high boots. I wasn't really a gentleman, although Dame Hermengilde had always taught me to be one, and I couldn't help noticing the pantaloons, as Annot had taken off her skirt and most of her petticoats. She was trying to wring the water out of them by rolling and pressing them on the rocks. Her curling hair was pulled into a tight braid, from which frizzy ends sprang out, making her head look, in the golden candlelight, like she trailed a cloud of gold dust. Her eyebrows and her mouth had a quirk of humor, but her eyes were sad.

When she saw me watching, she glared. "Are you looking at my legs?" she demanded.

"No," I said. "Well, yes. Why aren't ladies supposed to show their legs? You still have more clothes on than me."

"How should I know?" she snapped, but then she grinned. "I guess you poor men just find ankles too exciting."

"What about knees?"

Annot threw a rolled-up petticoat at me.

"Annot," I asked then, clutching the petticoat, "what you said in the Hall of Judgement…did Chancellor Holden really murder your mother?"

The baroness sat back on her heels.

"Yes," she said. Then she added, "I don't know. I believe he did, but I can't prove it. I knew they were my father's cousins, Chancellor Holden and Master Arvol, but we never saw them. He didn't get along with them. They lived here in Cragroyal, and my father never liked coming to the city. He liked to be out in the woods, hunting, or on the hills with his shepherds, but he wasn't one of those men that only think about hunting and drinking, you know. He was educated here at Cragroyal in Chrysanthemum College. We had an observatory in an old watchtower. He'd take me up there at night and teach me all the names of the stars and the constellations, show me how the planets moved. Have you ever seen the moon through a telescope, Maurey? There are mountains on it and great seas of shadow."

"I've seen illustrations," I said.

"I'll show you the real thing, if I ever get back to my observatory and my telescope," Annot promised. "Anyway, my father's cousins called him a backwoods boor, and he called them city dandies. After he died—he caught a chill, out helping the men look for lost sheep in a sleet storm—Holden and Arvol came up to Oakhold. They wanted to bring me south to the court here in Cragroyal, to make a lady of me, they said. My mother wouldn't agree. Holden takes the Hallalander view of women, you know. He thinks our minds are feeble and that we should be treated as children all our lives. He thinks we shouldn't ever be able to inherit important things, like land and titles, in our own right. So he thought both that he should have been my guardian after my father died, and that he should have been Baron of Oakhold himself. Anyway, when my mother refused their claim to me, Arvol went back to Cragroyal but Holden stayed, and then my mother fell ill. Our own physician couldn't diagnose the sickness for certain. It was like stomach fever or bad water, but she was the only one sick, so he said she must have a growth in her stomach. He was so impressed, having the great Master Holden there, that he left all her treatment to the chancellor. She was horribly sick. It went on and on for about six weeks, her getting sicker and then better and then sicker again. Vomiting and cramps, and, well—it wasn't nice. And she died. It was some foul magic, I think. Or poison."

"I'm sorry," I said.

"At her funeral I promised her shade I'd make them pay, someday," Annot said, matter-of-factly. She touched the center of her chest; then she fished a damp silk bag out of the neck of her shift. It was hung on a dark-blue ribbon, and I was reminded of the chain I'd worn with my mother's rings. She held the little bag the same way I'd sometimes held the rings, praying to my mother's shade—as firmly and tenderly as if it were a mother's hand.

"This is a lock of her hair," she said and unknotted the bag to show me.

It wasn't a delicate snip of hair, but a long, slender chestnut-brown braid, coiled up and tied with another dark-blue mourning ribbon.

I wasn't sure what to say. People often did keep locks of hair as memorials of someone they loved, but it didn't seem right to say, "Oh, that's nice," or some other meaningless thing.

"You must miss her," I said.

Annot put the memento of her mother away.

"I miss them both. More than you—well, you do know. You've lost everyone who matters too. You understand. When I was small I used to wish I was grown up and on my own. I was going to live off by myself in one of the manor houses or maybe travel to Rona on the continent, see a bit of the world. Not have parents telling me what to do..." She shrugged and started thumping the rolled-up skirts on the stones again, watching the water trickle down to the river.

"Anyway, once my mother was dead, Cousin Holden had his way and brought me down to Cragroyal, and I had to start dressing like a porcelain doll, to be dangled in front of the king like a worm on a hook."

"Why would they want you to marry the king?" I asked. The king. King Dugald. My brother, Dugald. I couldn't make the words seem real. *My brother.* "I mean, of course everyone would like their daughter or whatever to marry the king, but why would they murder for it? Why is it so important to them?"

"Well, you've seen Dugald," Annot said. "He's a nice man. He's fairly intelligent. He's kind. He's…sort of sweet, I guess. But all his life, even before King Burrage died, Cousin Holden's always been right there, telling Dugald what to do, what to say, what to think. Holden was Dugald's tutor, you know. So Dugald doesn't have much backbone. Holden never let him develop one. But someday he might start thinking for himself, or he might marry a woman who wouldn't like him being told what to do all the time by his Chief Minister. I think my cousins think that if I marry the king, they can go on telling us both what to do. Or even..."

"What?"

Annot shrugged again. "They've already killed my mother. It wouldn't surprise me if, well, if Dugald and I were married, and had a baby, then Dugald would get sick and die, or maybe we both would, and Cousin Holden would be the baby king or queen's guardian, being its cousin and the Chief Minister. And he'd have twenty-one years to rule the kingdom, before the baby came of age. And twenty-one years to make it a docile, obedient puppet, even more than Dugald is."

"I can't imagine any child of yours being docile and obedient," I said, and Annot laughed.

"Yes, my father always said anyone could guess I was born under the star of Vepris of the Wilderness, though he didn't really believe such things shaped a person. Cousin Holden might get a nasty surprise if the baby took after me. But it isn't going to happen, because here we are, on the way to Talverdin."

"Yes," I said slowly. "About that..."

"Where else can we go?"

I didn't have any suggestions.

"Anyway, don't you think they should be warned about that ring that has Cousin Holden so excited?"

After a while we went on, down the river. The baroness carried the lantern, which cast a pool of dim golden light and prevented me from seeing much better than she could unless I looked away from the glow. It also prevented her tripping on the uneven shelves of stone.

Blaze trotted ahead, his tail wagging gently. The river began to flow more quickly, foaming over its shelving bed, swirling into little whirlpools. In places the roof dropped almost to the level of our heads, and the wall leaned in, forcing us to edge gingerly along narrow ledges—the river was too deep and swift here for either wading or swimming. Once or twice I saw a sudden whirl and splash, as a tiny lake-seal's head disappeared under the water, alarmed at the sight of people along the secret river.

"I see light," Annot said, after a while. She hid the lantern behind her back, and we both peered ahead. With the light of the lantern shielded, I could see the glow of the rocks and the water clearly again. I could also see what Annot saw: the gleam of distant sunlight slipping around the farthest ledge.

We settled down to wait until sunset, before venturing out of the river's tunnel. Annot blew out her candle. We didn't dare make a fire, so we huddled together under a blanket, shivering, with only our body heat to dry our clothes. Blaze kept trying to head out into the sunlight, so eventually Annot put a leash on him. We both fell asleep.

When I awoke, the baroness was cuddled up against me, her head on my shoulder. I put my arm around her, very carefully so that she wouldn't wake up. She sighed and snuggled closer, and I fell asleep again, perfectly happy despite my cold wet clothes and the throbbing pain of my fingers and ankles. When I awoke for a second time it was because Annot was shaking me.

"It must be night," she said. "Time to go on, Maurey."

We ate another meal there by the river's edge, but whether to call it breakfast or supper, I couldn't decide. Blaze gobbled his share of the oatcakes and cold greasy sausages and whined. It probably didn't seem like much of a meal for a big dog.

"Rabbits," Annot told him. "We'll have rabbits as soon as we're into the forest. Maybe even a deer."

"How?" I asked. I wasn't thinking very clearly, after the last two days of terror and hunger.

Annot snorted. "I have sinew for snares. I came prepared. And did you think my bow was only for being Fuallin-Queen in a pageant?"

"No," I said humbly. I remembered Fuallin-Day and Harvest pageants back at Dame Hermengilde's. A young couple from the village would be chosen to act the roles of Jock Wildwood and Fuallin-Queen, dressed all in green and gold, garlanded with spring flowers or autumn nuts and barley. Sometimes the Fuallin-Queen carried a bow, but it was always a child's toy, wrapped around with flowers. She never even pretended to hunt anything with it, though the Fuallin-month Queen was none other than the Great Power Vepris of the Wild made tame, according to the scholars.

Annot felt around for my hand and patted it. "Eat," she said. "You need your strength. I'll shoot you a pheasant as soon as we're in the forest. I just hope you know how to cook it."

"Or gut it," I said, gloomily.

"Oh, I can do that." Annot sounded very cheerful at the prospect. "It's the actual cooking I never learned."

When we had eaten, I led the way onwards, holding Annot's hand. It was a long, thin, delicate hand. I could feel every slender bone. It was difficult to concentrate on picking the smoothest path—my awareness was all on Annot's touch until I stumbled and tripped, pulling us both down.

"What is it?" Annot asked, feeling around and whacking me in the ear with her elbow. "What happened? Are you all right?"

My face burned. "Just a loose rock," I muttered, picking up Blaze's leash and putting it back in her other hand. "Sorry."

We went on, and I kept my mind on my feet. In a short time we were squeezing around a great water-rounded knob of rock on our hands and knees, with the river licking us and a tangled curtain of ivy, which scrambled over the rock arch of the river's mouth, hanging down to claw at our hair and dip tendrils in the current. We were out of Cragroyal, safe on the shores of Cragfoot Lake, from which the River Beldain ran east to the sea. I wondered what the name of the underground river that fed the lake was, and where it sprang from. How far had the waters traveled before they found their way to the light, and what secrets might the Beldain carry away to lose in the restless ocean? I think I was a little delirious. Over our heads, the white stars burned, reflecting in the black water as if their twins swam there in the depths.

Annot took a deep breath, freeing her hand from mine, and Blaze shook himself vigorously.

"Onwards," the baroness said. "We'd better get into the forest before dawn."

"Aren't you tired?" I asked. I was exhausted, despite having slept twice in the cave. I could hardly bear the thought of going on, of walking into the unknown, with no goal but the deadly, enchanted Talverdin Mountains to look forward to, and a horrible death waiting if we failed in our mad plan.

Annot was silent. Then she said, "If I stop to think or rest I'm going to start bawling like a baby, Maurey." Her voice shook a little. "So..." She climbed to her feet and struck a grand pose, like the statue of conquering King Hallow landing on the shores of Eswiland, the one that stands in the formal garden of the palace. She pointed westwards with her bow like he did with his sword. "Onwards, my heroes." She twitched at Blaze's leash. "That means you, boy. On your paws."

She was quite right. We couldn't afford to sit around feeling sorry for ourselves. We would have to indulge in self-pity while we walked.

I stood up, feeling stiff and sore and about sixty years old. When I tugged the pack off her shoulders and slung it over my own, she said nothing, but she smiled at me in the darkness. I tried to grin back, even though she probably couldn't see more than the vague shadow of me in the starlight.

"Onwards," I agreed, and led the way along the shore, heading for where the highway ran beside it. We should be able to follow the highway for a mile or two and then take one of the crossing byways into the great Westwood, the forest that covered most of the foothills of the Talverdin Mountains and sent long fingers out to the east, even as far as Cragroyal.

Blaze, pulling forwards at my side, suddenly stopped and growled deep in his chest, looking off towards the highway, which was hidden from us by its hedges and the steeply dropping lakeshore.

"Blaze, quiet," Annot hissed, but at the same moment she stumbled over a stone and it slid, rattling and clinking.

"Down there!" a man shouted. "Stay where you are, in the king's name!"

In a blaze of orange light, someone carrying a torch moved from behind a dense stand of yews. More came behind him. In the torchlight they were a crowd of black shadows, packed close together, forcing their way through the bushes.

"You've nothing to fear, if you've honest business on the lake," one called to us. "But you'd be better off inside than eel fishing tonight. There's a warlock abroad!"

"Stay where you are!" the first voice shouted again. "Come into the light where we can see you!"

"Which?" shouted Annot. "Stay where we are or come into the light? We're only poor eel fishers, me 'n my brother, and all your noise is going to scare 'em away."

That didn't stop the soldiers. She probably hadn't believed that it would. She wrapped Blaze's leash tighter around her hand, to stop him leaping up the bank at them.

"What now, Maurey?" she whispered. "They must be watching all around the city. If we run can we lose them in the dark?"

It was the only chance. We certainly couldn't fight them. But running would make noise. I tugged her hand and led the way up the shore, walking quickly and softly. Annot tugged Blaze along after her, holding her breath as though that would make her feet fall more quietly. The soldiers were coming down the bank with a great deal of crackling and crashing, and some cursing as they ran into a stand of hawthorns.

Maybe, I thought, we could hide until they had gone by. But they had torches, and Blaze kept trying to turn back, his teeth bared. He wouldn't keep quiet, if we had to hide. He was probably tired and hungry and as cranky as a dog could be.

I stared into the darkness, seeing every twig, every leaf, every stone on the shore, and no place that would let us disappear. The water rippled, black and velvet green and silver, and a spray of wild roses nodded, glowing faintly pink, like a shy blush. Then I saw more yew trees, halfway up the bank. They were dark trees, their soft needles nearly black even in daylight, and these were a knotted, snarled tangle, their limbs wrapping around one another as if they held some ancient secret hidden within. It was the best we could do. Behind us, the soldiers shouted, tumbling down onto the shore, their boots clattering on the stones.

"That way!" one shouted. "It's the warlock; it must be. Eel fishers wouldn't run."

"You sure he can't get into the halfworld?" another gasped, panting. He sounded like a fat man. "No point chasing him if he's already gone."

"His Honor the Chancellor said he was wounded, too sick to hardly stand. Said we'd catch him easy. Come on!"

We pushed our way into the deepest blackness, the heart of the yews. Annot dropped to her knees, holding Blaze's jaw shut. The dog quivered but didn't whine. I tried to slow my breathing, quiet my pounding heart, as though the soldiers would be able to hear it drumming. I tried to be nothing but shadow within the shadow of the trees, so that if they looked, they would see nothing, go on past. And the world faded to gray around me, as it had when I hid in the wine cellar.

"They've gone back up the bank!"

I heard the soldiers, but as though they were far off, muffled in fog. I saw Annot looking around, her hair no longer gleaming as it did when I saw it in darkness, but a faint, pearly gray. She reached out with the hand that didn't hold Blaze, feeling for me.

I felt her, a distant cold touch, like the breath of fog. But she obviously felt nothing, for she flailed around wildly, and her face was panicked.

I reached to her, caught her hand, and drew her and the dog both into the halfworld after me. I don't know how I knew, in that moment, the way to do it. I just did it.

Annot clung to me, blinking. I rather enjoyed that.

"I can see," she whispered. "Sort of. It's gone all foggy. Maurey, you just disappeared. Are we—we're in the halfworld, aren't we?"

"Shh," I said. I didn't know if the soldiers would hear us. I didn't actually think they could. But, as I said, I was enjoying, for just one moment, being the sort of strong commanding man that women cling to.

Annot pushed me away, not letting go of my hand, though.

"Don't look so smug," she whispered. "I bet you didn't do it on purpose. You said you couldn't."

"Well," I said, "at least I brought *you* here on purpose. Come on. Let's get away while we're still here."

"What happens if I let go of your hand?"

"I don't know."

Annot took a tighter grip on both me and Blaze's leash.

To tell the truth, as the soldiers came closer I found I was just as afraid of them as I had been when we were creeping along the lakeshore. I didn't know anything about the halfworld. I'd only ever gone there by accident and still didn't know how I did it or how I came back. But if we sat in the yew trees waiting for the soldiers to go away, sooner or later we would tumble out of the halfworld again, and if the soldiers hadn't gone, they would find us. They were beating through all the bushes now, torches held high.

The halfworld was a strange place, a land of shadows and fog, echoing the real world. Rocks and earth were solid under our feet, but reaching to bend a spray of ivy out of my way, my hand passed right through it, with only a cool misty feeling over my skin. The older trees were more substantial than saplings. It seemed the younger something was, the foggier, less real, it felt.

Later I learned that though this was true, use and purpose could also give something solidity in the halfworld, even something made of young, new materials. At the time all I knew was that though we walked through the ivy and grass without a betraying ripple, the tree roots could still trip us. It was a dream-world with the unreality of a fever-dream, and it gave me a bit of the same edge-of-panic feeling I had in my nightmares the time that I fell ill with the sweating ague, as though the familiar world had been whisked away and replaced with some imperfect forgery. Only the stars overhead were the same.

We walked down the edge of the highway, and another troop of soldiers, these ones mounted, rode wearily back towards the city as though they had been searching for a day and night. They passed right by us. One or two of the horses rolled their eyes and laid their ears back as if seeing ghosts, but none of the soldiers saw anything at all.

We walked, and every time the gray world started to waver around us I thought of darkness, of night's shadow wrapped around us close and safe as a blanket, and the world stayed gray.

The sun came up, a dim white light, but there were still stars, constellations that were wrong for this time of the year, but of course, the stars were there in the daylight world too, only unseen in the sun's light. More travelers came on to the highway, farmers heading to village markets, and in the jostling crowds we remained as insubstantial as ghosts. Blaze whined and pressed himself against Annot's legs, frightened, poor beast. I found it unsettling too, though I wouldn't have admitted it to Annott, and at the first chance, I led off onto a narrow trail heading west, towards the shadowy forest.

There, under the sheltering trees, I felt the halfworld slipping away from me. I clutched after it, but the gray world was gone, and the sun-dappled green of the forest engulfed us. My eyes were so heavy I could no longer hold them open, and I sank down to sleep in the first fern-filled hollow we came to.

Part Two

✤ Chapter Seven ✤
The King's Men

In the days that followed, as we wandered deeper and deeper into Westwood, I never found my way to the halfworld again, no matter how hard I tried to push my way in, no matter how black the shadow I tried to merge with. And I knew we could not be lucky forever. Some time they were going to catch up, and we would need the halfworld to hide.

We had several close calls. King's messengers passed us four or five times, probably carrying word of our escape to those few villages that lay within the forest itself, or to barons at their hunting lodges. We usually heard them coming, and the dull thud of hooves on the beaten earth of the trail, the jingle of harness, was enough of a warning. After the first time or two that we hurried into the undergrowth to hide, Annot with her hands around Blaze's muzzle, the dog seemed to learn that we needed to avoid people. He would grow anxious, pricking his ears and growling in the direction from which a rider was coming, long before our mere human hearing told us of danger. There were pedlars and chapmen to hide from too, tramping along with their goods on their backs, woodsmen on their way from cottage to clearing, axe on shoulder, and hunters. We feared the hunters most, men—and a few women, I was surprised to see, but I had been too long in the city, and forgot that in the wilds, traditions of who could do what were not so rigid—who could read the forest, and who had dogs with them more often than not. A bent twig, a bruised fern, might give us away, if their dogs' noses did not. But we were lucky, or Annot's woodscraft was as good as she claimed. No hunter ever came peering into our hiding places, and Blaze was a peaceable dog, who only wagged his tail in a friendly fashion when some hound thrust its head into the bracken to sniff at us.

It was Therminas, month of the summer solstice, and life in the Westwood was good on the sunny days. In the rain it was miserable. Annot had a hooded cloak for herself of tightly woven, oily wool, but I made do with a blanket. We didn't travel when it rained. If you have a roof and a fireplace and dry clothes waiting for you, rain is nothing to worry about, but if all you have to look forward to is a cold wet night, back to back under a wet blanket, and no dry wood for a fire, that's a different matter entirely. On rainy days we found the best shelter we could, a dense spruce tree, perhaps, or a cedar, and once a real cave, and kept ourselves and what wood we could find as dry as possible. We knew that if either of us fell ill, living in this way, the chances were we would never recover. But Sypat favored us, and we neither took a chill. Or perhaps Vepris of the Wild protected Annot and overlooked me for her sake. She certainly seemed to me like one of the wild maidens the old myths said had attended the Power of the Wilds, when that Lady roamed the earth in far-off days.

Annot knew as much about gathering wild plants for food as any forest hunter, though her method of cooking both roots and greens was to simmer everything into a sort of slurry in her kettle and call it stew. After the first of our heated arguments—of which we had one about every day, till we realized that neither of us was actually trying to insult the other by saying we had a better idea about which way to go or what to do—I took over all the cooking. I might not have known what the plants were called, or where to find them, but from years of living in a kitchen I had a far better idea than she did of how not to turn everything to tasteless mush. Annot might say she longed for fresh bread and spiced pies, but I had not eaten so well in years. *Meat*—I had been lucky to get the cold gristly scraps that were scraped off the plates for the turnspit dog. Hot meat, sizzling over the fire, was all I needed to feel we were feasting every night. Annot was a better shot than many of the king's huntsmen, she claimed, and from what I saw I believed her. She shot grouse and pheasants and snared rabbits when we camped for the night. Several times she shot a deer, and even Blaze was able to eat his fill. When she took a deer, we cooked and carried all the meat we could, as much as we thought would keep till we ate it, but still had to leave part of the carcass for the wolves. I would have felt utterly useless, except that I remembered Harl Steward teaching me to fish, back when I was a little boy at Dame Hermengilde's, so once we acquired fishhooks, I was able to help feed us as well. We didn't get those fishhooks without effort, though.

Annot was keen on disguise. Soon after we entered the forest, she gathered a bag of unripe walnuts from a black walnut tree we camped under, and steeped a greenish brown juice from their sticky aromatic husks, to paint my face and hands with. I protested that this dye made me look green, like some sort of plague victim, but Annot insisted it gave my skin the olive-brown cast of someone from Rona on the continent.

I held my fresh-dyed hands out before me, frowning at them. "I must look like one of those trolls they say people worship instead of the Powers, in Gehtaland and the other barbarian countries in the north." I meant the north of the continent, not the north of our island of Eswiland, of course. I might have only had two years of schooling, but I was not so ignorant as that. "We won't have to worry about anyone finding out who we are. They'll take one look and run screaming."

"With your black hair it looks perfectly natural," Annot said, frowning at her own hands. She had used the same dye to turn her hair a drab mousy brown, but had forgotten to protect her skin. She shrugged. "I suppose we're so dirty no one will notice that my hands are too dark."

But for days after that we continued to hide whenever Blaze warned us of another's approach. We both felt that Cragroyal was still too close. I grumbled that the dye was a wasted effort, particularly when Annot decided I needed a second treatment.

However, deep within the Westwood, where the people of the few isolated steadings traveled to the nearest village only once or twice a year, we were not so afraid of meeting strangers. At one woodsman's cottage Annot spun a tale of how I was her cousin, born of an aunt who went to Korharbor to work as a servant and "got herself in trouble" with a Ronish sailor. We were on our way to live with a grandmother in the west. Her fine dress? Oh, a cast-off from the aunt's mistress. Wasn't it lovely? To earn my precious fishhooks, I split wood all one afternoon for the elderly wife while Annot weeded her garden. Coin would have raised suspicions in such a place, but honest labor won us trust and sympathy. I was not used to receiving either; it hurt to think it was only due to the walnut husks. The old woman reminded me of Dame Hermengilde. At another cottage, Annot carded wool while I shoveled the winter's dung from the sheep shed. Our payment was a pair of shoes and a moth-eaten blanket. At a third, we weeded the kale field in the burning sun for a suit of clothes—shirt and woollen hose and peasant's smock—outgrown by a son and not so badly worn as the ones falling apart on my back.

With the fishhooks and a length of fine twine I caught trout in the swiftly flowing brooks, bass and the occasional fierce pike in the little lakes. We had food, sweet water to drink, clothes, wood to burn and trees (better than nothing) to shelter us from the rain—almost everything we needed, it seemed.

"I wish we could just go on living like this," I burst out one evening. "I've never..."

Annot looked up from checking over her sinew snares, surprised, I think, by how angry I sounded. I was surprised myself. I hadn't realized, until that moment, how happy I was and how little I wanted things to change. I didn't want to get to Talverdin.

"Never what?" she asked.

I shrugged. "Never been so happy. Not since I was little."

"Oh." It looked oddly as though Annot was blushing. "Well," she said, "I'm glad I rescued you, then."

"Don't you ever wish you hadn't? I mean, you're a baroness! You've got a great hall..."

"A castle, actually."

"And land. Horses and silver and servants."

"A library," she said, a bit wistfully, "and an observatory, in the old tower. I miss my telescope."

"Don't you wish you were back there?"

"Well, if I hadn't rescued you, I wouldn't be back there anyway. I'd still be stuck in Cragroyal, with my dear cousins Holden and Arvol dangling me in front of your brother like a worm on a hook. Anyway, being Baroness of Oakhold isn't about silver and servants. It's about the kingdom, about Dunmorra. Being a baron means serving the king and the kingdom, and the kingdom is the people. And that doesn't mean doing what Cousin Holden says I should and letting innocent Nightwalkers get burned to death. It means doing what is right. That's what my father always said. The barons must protect their people, serve justice and be loyal to the king. And the king must be just and fair. When the king doesn't do what is right, what is just—then the king is wrong."

"Ah," I said, thinking of how Dugald had protested so feebly when Chancellor Holden talked of executing me. I wondered what he had been told being a king meant.

"Of course," Annot said, "my father also said I was born to be a poacher. Come and help me set these snares."

It does not take so very long to cross the Westwood, of course, even on its twisting paths, but that is if you know where you are going. In fine weather with dry trails, a king's messenger on horseback can travel from Cragroyal northwest to Greyrock Town in a week. We were not exactly lost, but our course, which should have taken us west and north, wandered. Sometimes I know we went in circles, losing our bearings when neither sun nor stars could be seen for the clouds. We had to go around lakes, seek fords over the little rivers, avoid the rare villages, where people were more likely to ask questions about who we were, and less likely to be satisfied with Annot's story of the aunt and the Ronish sailor. Besides, we were in no particular haste.

Sometimes we camped for as many as four or five days in one place, before fear of discovery drove us on. It was easy to forget why we had decided we had to reach Talverdin. More and more often, I found myself looking at the land, especially along the ravines where the maples and elms and pines climbed broken cliffs, and thinking that if we could find a cave, we could make ourselves a home. Live in the Westwood forever, as I wished, hunting and foraging, a cross between outlaws and hermits and forest-steaders. But my dream of a peaceful forest life, forgetting all the dangers of the outer world, vanished like morning mist one day, when we had been in the Westwood for well over a month.

I had persuaded Annot we should follow a narrow brook along the bottom of a ravine, picking our way over broken stone, struggling through scratchy teasel and crushing mint beneath our feet. There was a path, but it looked rarely used and that suited me. I was secretly looking for caves again. When Blaze turned to face behind us, hackles rising and a growl rumbling deep in his chest, I at first thought of bear or wolves—we had seen no sign of humans for several days. Annot thought the same. She was stringing her bow even as I held up a hand.

"Listen! Horses?"

Annot froze, straining to hear. The sound grew louder. Not just one horse, but the clatter of many hooves, echoing off the sides of the ravine. A group of horsemen in the Westwood was not going to be a party of merchants or pilgrims. Then came the sound of a man's voice, raised. "This can't be the way. We should have followed the other branch of the stream."

"It's the straightest route to Greyrock Town, sir. I served with the Greyrock Castle garrison, and this is the route the messengers took when they were in a hurry. A ravine, they said, cutting between the southern trail and the northerly. That's what you said you wanted."

Annot slacked the string off her bow and put Blaze's leash on him, her mouth grim. I shouldered the pack, and we both looked around for the best place to hide. The sides of the ravine here were almost cliffs. Climbing the crumbling ledges of rock beside us was a patch of the vicious, razor-thorned shrub called prickly ash. It was dense enough to hide in but cut through cloth and sliced flesh. Only desperation made any creature larger than a rabbit crawl through prickly ash.

We were desperate.

"You go ahead," Annot whispered, "so I can untangle the pack when you get stuck. Take Blaze."

No time to argue. I took the dog's leash and urged him ahead of me, following on hands and knees. From outside the prickly ash looked like a single plant, a mound of greenery, but it was actually a miniature forest of slender stems. I squeezed between the trunks, trying to keep from brushing against the branches. Twigs caught in my hair; thorns ripped my skin and tore my clothes. Then what Annot had feared happened. The pack caught against a branch, and I was stuck.

"Geneh damn it," Annot cursed as I tried to free myself from the strap over my shoulder without flaying my face. She hissed, tearing her hand on the thorns. Blaze tried to turn back to see what was keeping us and tangled his leash around a stem.

"Stay!" I whispered, before he made it any worse.

It was dark under the prickly ash, on the shadowed side of the ravine. Maybe, I thought, and tried, without any great hope, to find my way into the halfworld again. Into the shadow, I thought. I'm going to dissolve into the shadow. But after so many failures I couldn't even pretend much hope. Besides, even hope would not admit that this was very dark.

"You're free—go," said Annot, shoving at my rump.

"You! Up there!"

We both froze. I grabbed Blaze around the muzzle. "No! Quiet!"

He whined but did not bark.

"Come down. I want to talk to you."

Annot scrambled up practically on top of me, and we stared at one another wide-eyed.

"Don't make me come up to get you."

Annot swallowed. "You stay here with Blaze. I'll be all right."

"You can't."

"No choice." She gave me a bold smile, but it looked a bit forced. "It'll be fine, so long as they don't see *you*. Walnut dye won't fool this bunch, not with those black eyes of yours."

She began to back out. I managed to get the pack off and left it, crawling a few feet after her, keeping Blaze close. Annot was already out, standing at the edge of the bushes to call, "What do you want?" The first thing I saw was a banner, snapping in the wind. Just as we had feared—black tower outlined in silver rays on a blue field, the emblem of the king. Following came a good two-dozen riders, royal men-at-arms, with their servants and packhorses behind them.

"Just some cottager," said a man riding at the fore. "Nothing to worry about, sir."

Annot bobbed a hasty curtsey. She did not look much like a cottager to me, but she did not look much like the Baroness of Oakhold either. Her green dress was stained dark with mud and ground-in bark and ashes. Her skin was not much better, and though the walnut dye had been used up some weeks ago, her hair was still a streaked tawny color, too grubby for the fading dye and coppery roots to show. Her face and hands were bleeding from fresh scratches, scabby with old ones.

"Excellent," said the captain, "because this route is no good, no good at all. Perfect place for an ambush. There's got to be a better road, and we need local help to find it."

"But sir—"

"We'll cut a new road over the high ground. There's no way His Grace the Chancellor will lead an army through here. You! Get down here!" The captain beckoned to Annot. "Hurry up, girl. We mean you no harm."

Annot curtsied again, another quick bob, not a proper court curtsey. "Stay here," she muttered, without moving her lips. "I'll be fine. Keep Blaze quiet."

She began picking her way down the side of the ridge, skidding on loose rock, keeping her eyes timidly on her feet.

"Sir?" she said meekly, with yet another bob, stopping when she was halfway down.

"What are you doing up there, girl?"

"Looking for my goat, sir. You haven't seen her, have you? She's a flop-eared black, sir, and the best milker we have."

"No, I haven't seen your goat. You're from the village?"

We hadn't known there was a village nearby.

Annot hesitated only a second. Then she curtsied again. "No, sir. I live with my gran."

"And where does your gran live?"

"That way, sir." Annot waved a hand vaguely south and curtsied yet again. "A long ways, sir. But I can't find my goat."

"Well, we haven't seen it. And we haven't eaten it."

The captain was obviously trying to make a joke, to set the peasant girl at her ease. Annot just hunched her shoulders.

"Listen, girl. We want to find a way to—what's the next village?"

I felt as though my heart stopped, but he wasn't asking Annot.

The man beside him answered.

"Hollyside."

"To Hollyside. We want to get to Hollyside."

"You just keep on going, sir," Annot said.

"No, we want a better way. One that doesn't go crawling between the rocks like this."

"But this is the way, sir," said Annot. "It's the only way I know."

"Listen," the captain said patiently. "Do you know about the warlock?"

"Warlock, sir?"

"The one that stole the king's bride, the chancellor's niece, earlier this summer."

"Oh, that warlock. Yes, sir. Everyone's heard about that."

"Well, Chancellor Holden, who is a very great man in Cragroyal, a very wise and learned man and King Dugald's chief advisor, has found a way to defeat the evil magic of the Nightwalkers. He's going to lead an army to Talverdin and destroy the warlocks once and for all. We're trying to find the best route for the army to come by next spring. Do you understand?"

"Yes, sir," said Annot. "But this is the way to Hollyside."

"Stupid peasant," said the man who had been giving directions. "We know that."

The captain muttered something to him, and the man scowled.

"What we want to know," the captain went on patiently, "is if there's any other track that goes towards Hollyside and on to Greyrock Town on the edge of the mountains. It doesn't have to be a road, just a track. The king will hire foresters to clear it this autumn. Maybe you have brothers who'd like to work for the king, making the road?"

"They're dead, sir," said Annot. "But I think there's a track that goes around the other side of that big hill to the north. My gran said there was. But it might be gone now. I don't know."

"Can you show us?"

"I don't know where it is, sir. I just heard about it."

"Could your gran show us?"

"No!" Annot curtsied again. "I mean, no, sir. She's very old sir, and her mind wanders."

"Well, you come along with us and show us where you think it is, and there'll be a silver penny for you. And we'll keep an eye out for your goat."

"But sir..."

"Come along down, girl. We don't have all day. I give you my word you'll come to no harm by us."

Annot went scrambling and sliding down to the bottom of the ravine, deliberately clumsy. Rocks clattered and rattled down around her, covering the noise of Blaze whining. I gripped his collar with both hands and whispered, "Quiet!" into his ear, pulling him back against myself. Annot had dropped her bow in the bushes before she crawled out. I had a wild thought, myself shooting the captain, us escaping up the cliff. It was a very stupid thought.

Her bow was here, but her quiver was hanging from her belt! No peasant girl would be out seeking a lost goat with a huntsman's quiver of arrows on her.

Then I saw it. In all her bobbing of curtsies she had managed to unbuckle her belt and drop it.

"What's your name?" the captain asked.

"Allie, sir," Annot said.

"You'll ride behind me and tell me the way, Allie. Don't be afraid of the horse. She's very friendly."

"Yes, sir," said Annot, and a soldier dismounted. He picked her up around the waist and heaved her up behind the captain, with a grin and a comment about hanging on good and tight.

Annot gave a squeak of alarm, like a peasant girl who'd never ridden a horse before, and clutched the captain.

I hoped and prayed to all the Powers that they didn't know enough about women's fashions to notice that her dress, stained and torn though it was, was a lady's riding attire and not a peasant's shorter skirts. Or that her boots were very expensive, not wooden clogs or shoes homemade from a single square of leather, folded and laced. Besides, any peasant girl would be going barefoot in the middle of summer. But they didn't seem to notice. People in general aren't very observant, in my experience. I took a couple of deep breaths, trying to think calmly. Although they might have been told to keep an eye out for the missing baroness while they scouted a road to the Greyrock Pass, they should not be too suspicious unless they knew her well. I suppose to the men-at-arms, who would never have seen her except as the pale dainty lady with the red-gold curls, the grubby, tanned, dull-haired girl with the scratched and scabby hands and face of a poacher was a completely different person. I could barely remember how delicate and ethereal she had seemed, back before I got to know her.

I watched as the cavalcade got itself turned around and rode back the way it had come, with Annot clinging to the captain at its head.

Blaze whined again. Annot never looked back.

When they were out of sight, I gathered up the bow and

Annot's belt and quiver, and slung the pack on my back. Then I climbed the rest of the way to the top of the ridge and settled down among the maples and ashes to wait.

It was a very long afternoon.

The sun was just setting when a whistle made Blaze leap to his feet and start barking.

"There you are." I hadn't seen or heard Annot coming through the tangled undergrowth, but there she was, moving silent as a poacher through the sumac and honeysuckle thickets. She nearly fell as the dog flung himself at her. I was just as relieved.

"What happened? Why were you gone so long?"

"It's a long way around to the other side of that damned hill," Annot said, collapsing onto the moss. "Ick, not my ear, Blaze. Take your tongue away. And then we had to find the track."

"What track?"

"The track my gran told me about, of course. The one that goes to Hollyside."

"You don't have a gran."

"Everyone has a gran, Maurey. Everyone has two, actually. Even you."

I tossed a pebble at her. She grinned. "Those poor men-at-arms. I almost feel sorry for them. They searched and searched and kept saying, 'Is it here? Didn't your gran tell you where it began? Think, girl!' And then we found it."

"Really?"

"Well, it was a track on the north side of the hill, anyway. It didn't look like it had been used for years, all overgrown. It probably went to some forester's holding once, but it's just a deer trail now. Anyway, they were so happy, you'd think we'd found a paved highway with a milestone saying 'This way to Talverdin.' And then they wanted me to go all the way on to Hollyside with them."

"How did you get away?"

"I cried."

"You cried?"

"Yes," said Annot, with great dignity. "That's a woman's last weapon, you know. Or one of them." She grinned. "Knees and elbows didn't seem called for."

"Annot!"

"They were really quite nice boys, except for that one who called me a stupid peasant. Anyway, I cried. I said I had to get home to my gran and she'd be so upset and I still hadn't found the goat. So the captain gave me a hanky and a silver tuppence. Do you think I can afford to buy a new goat?"

"Annot!"

"What, you don't think we need a goat?"

"Annot..." I gave up. "Should we go on, or do you want to camp here?"

"I don't want to walk another step. But I suppose we'd better move away from the ravine, just in case they get lost and come back here. It's a good thing I dyed my hair," she added. "I've seen a couple of those lads before, around the palace. Blaze would have given the game away."

"I'm surprised you didn't dye him too," I said, giving her a hand to pull herself up by.

"It would just make him look funny."

"Hah!" I said.

"Hah, what?"

"Hah, not like the rest of us. Come on. Let's find a place to camp. Maybe I'll catch some fish tonight."

Later that evening, three fat bass roasted in the coals, wrapped in wet ferns and clay, with watercress to flavor them.

"It smells wonderful," Annot said. "All those soldiers had to eat was oatcakes and jerky. Poor souls."

"They deserve it," I said. "Remember what they're doing."

"Yes." Annot snapped another stick and put it on the fire. "Cousin Holden is going to take an army to Talverdin next spring."

"Because of us. Or because he got that ring from me, anyway."

"Well, now we know where we are."

"Not that we were lost before."

"Of course not."

"But we do know the way to Greyrock Town now. If that path down below is the track the messengers follow, we can stay on it."

"We should be able to get to Talverdin before the month is out." Annot frowned. "Maybe sooner."

"Maybe longer," I said. "There's the mountains, don't forget."

"Well, we'll cross those when we come to them. At least we can warn the king, or whoever's in charge there, long before Cousin Holden can get his road built, and you can't move an army in winter."

"Warn them, if they'll listen to us," I said gloomily.

"I don't see why they wouldn't."

I watched the firelight flickering over her, striking highlights of gold from her hair where the walnut dye was fading.

* Chapter Eight *
The Bridge

We began to climb into the Talverdin Mountains several weeks later, at the end of the month of Melkinas, the month dedicated to Mayn as the guardian mother of beasts. It was supposed to be a month when no meat was eaten, but we could not afford such an indulgence and hunted as we always had. Mayn might or might not forgive us, Annot said, with cheerful irreverence, but Vepris the Huntress would understand. We could have made better time, but living off the land slows you down. Though we were more determined to steer a straight course now, we lost our way a few times too, mistaking the track.

The mountains had loomed over us for days, blue jagged peaks, gleaming with snow, glittering in the sun. Legend said there was a road through them, the Greyrock Pass. That was the way the Nightwalkers had fled. That was the way the human armies of King Hallow had pursued. And later, that was the way the survivors of those armies had stumbled back, broken and babbling of enchantment.

The Greyrock Pass was the way we would go. We didn't know of any other.

We hid in the trees on the edge of Greyrock Town's farmland, watching the troop of royal men-at-arms, tattered and draggled, riding past on the cart track.

"What happened to them?" I asked. "On a good track it shouldn't have taken them more than a few days, not more than a week, to get here from where we saw them. They had horses and supplies and that soldier who was supposed to know the Westwood to guide them."

"I guess my gran's path didn't go to Hollyside after all," Annot whispered. "But you know how forgetful old ladies can be."

"It's a pity they didn't stay lost a while longer," I whispered back. "What if they decide to check out the Greyrock Pass itself?"

"They won't," said Annot. "I'm sure even people from Greyrock don't go up there. I wouldn't, if I wasn't with you."

I wasn't so sure that my presence would help. I was only half Nightwalker. I imagined the Nightwalkers looking at me and shouting, "Human! Cut off his head!"

We crept around Greyrock Town's thick walls and beneath the high towers of Greyrock Castle in the middle of the night, and I found the track that climbed to the Greyrock Pass easily enough in the darkness. It was ancient. There was no sign that the townsfolk used it, even for taking their cattle up to the summer pastures on the mountainside.

"This was a highway once," Annot said, sliding her foot over smooth stones, laid together so skillfully that only in a few places was the road surface broken, the stones forced apart by trees. Moss crept over it along the edges, but the middle was still clear, a broad path of gleaming gray, shifting and shimmering like flowing water. "Maurey?"

I realized she had been speaking, while I stood entranced by the beauty of the stones.

"What do you see?"

"Water," I said, "like a calm river. I wish you could see what I do. It's all shadow and shimmer."

We stood there. I think we both felt that once we started walking on that road, there could be no turning back. For a moment I seemed to hear the sobbing ghosts of all the Dunmorran and Eswyn men who had died along its length, trying to cross into hidden Talverdin.

Annot called Blaze to her and fastened the leash to his collar, which she only did when there was some immediate danger, so I knew she was afraid too.

"Come on," I said and held out my hand. "We have to be out of sight of Greyrock Castle's towers by dawn, or your friends the men-at-arms will come to see if you've found your goat yet."

Annot took my hand, and we began to follow the silvery road as it climbed up into the mountains.

The road twisted and snaked beside a plunging stream for a time, and then turned away, rising steeply along the slope. To the left was a sheer drop, with nothing but a few scraggly spruces and larches to catch us if we fell. There was no reason we should fall off the edge of the road, not with my eyes, but just knowing the drop was there was enough to make me sweat.

The road climbed and climbed. In places it was nearly covered with shale and gravel that had washed down the mountainside from above. In others, creeping brambles covered it, clawing at our ankles and making Blaze whine and snap at his paws. Around midnight we stopped, made a fire, and had a late supper of cold pheasant stuffed with mushrooms and lambsquarter greens, and of course, oatcakes. I could hardly remember what bread tasted like. It was already colder than it had been down in the forest, and the road climbed higher still. We wrapped up in our blankets and lay one on either side of the fire, falling into the swift, deep sleep that long hours of physical labor bring.

No sooner was I asleep than I jerked awake again. With a sound like a baby's wail, the wind swept along the road. I could see it coming, shadowy shapes, mounted men in old-fashioned armor: short-sleeved mail-shirts, conical helmets. They rode over us while I blinked, not sure if I was awake or dreaming, and the fire went out like a snuffed candle. When I leaned over the ashes to shake Annot awake, they were cold.

I changed my mind and let her sleep. The knights might be the shades of the dead. They might be only illusion, part of the protection of the Greyrock Pass. Either way, I doubted they could harm us, and it had been a wearying climb, with miles still to go tomorrow. I muttered a hasty prayer to the Yerku, the warrior twins. If any Lesser Power had influence over these warrior shades, it would be the twins, the patrons of soldiers. Then, I settled to sleep again. If there was real danger, Blaze would wake us.

Dawn came, melting the frost that had settled over us in the night. Frost, while only a few hours' walk below men with scythes were heading for the hayfields! We had oatcakes and our last raisins for breakfast, and Blaze dug frenziedly at the side of the road, rooting out a mouse's nest and devouring the squeaking beasts. He didn't think much of stale oatcakes.

Annot was unusually silent.

"What's wrong?" I asked at last, when she had failed to laugh at some feeble joke.

She shrugged. "I didn't sleep well, I guess. Bad dreams."

"What sort of bad dreams?" I asked, almost afraid to know.

"I dreamed about King Hallow's knights," she said slowly. "They were dead. They were lying along the road, their bodies all bloody, and it was snowing, covering them up, and then the flowers came up through their bones. And they were there, their shades were there. They told me to go back. They said if I went on, I would die. Fescor would never find my shade, and I would haunt the mountains forever with them. They said...no human could survive, and I saw myself, saw my bones disappearing under moss, and my own ghost running along with the shades, up and down the highway, and the mountains closed around the road like a wall with no gates, and we could never get out, we can never get out..." Her voice shook.

"It's just a dream," I said. "Annot, it was just a dream. It must be part of the enchantments, the magic protecting the pass. It's only meant to frighten you, so you'll turn around and go back."

"It was so real," she said quietly.

"I know. But it was a dream. They just want to scare you."

"They certainly succeeded. You didn't dream at all?"

"No," I said finally. I had been awake when I saw the ghosts of Hallow's army. But I didn't think it would be helpful to mention that, somehow.

Annot gave me a weak smile. "It was awful. But I'm not going to be frightened into giving up now by a stupid dream. I'm sure the shades of King Hallow's knights have better things to do than haunt my dreams. Anyway, some of them were probably relatives."

"That shouldn't make you feel better, though," I said. "Look at how your relatives treat you."

That won a laugh from her, at last.

The day, which had begun in golden light, quickly grew gray and threatening. The wind began to blow with winter's bite. Rounding a buttress of rock, we saw far below us a foaming river.

There had been a bridge once; its piers were still visible, broken tumbles of rock rising from the steep valley.

Annot let out a stifled shriek and stumbled back. The road ended, crumbling away a mere yard in front of her. She crouched down and clutched Blaze as though he were an anchor.

I threw a rock and watched it fall. The splash of its landing was lost in the roar of the rapids below.

"Now what?" Annot asked, trying to sound cheerful. She didn't succeed. "We can't climb down there. Can we get around, do you suppose?"

I shook my head, watching the water.

"I think..." I shook my head again. "I think the bridge is still there, Annot."

Annot stared and swallowed. "Can you see it? That stone you threw didn't hit anything."

"I know."

But I *could* see the bridge, faint and elusive as a ghost in daylight. The road continued on, smooth and level, carried on three great arches of stone. I crawled to the very edge of the crumbled road and reached out a hand, my heart in my mouth.

Annot grabbed the back of my belt.

My hand went right through the ghostly roadbed.

"It's not there," I said. I had been so certain it was.

"But you can see it?" Annot tugged on my belt. "Come back. Just seeing you so close to the edge is making me sick to my stomach."

We sat side by side. Across the gorge the highway continued, enticingly near, impossibly distant.

"But I *can* see it," I said. "It's like fog, like a ghost."

"When have you ever seen a ghost?" Annot muttered, glumly throwing a rock herself. "I'm the one having nightmares."

"It's like how people seem when I'm in the halfworld."

"Oh," said Annot. "Have you been able to get into the halfworld lately?"

"No." I hadn't tried in weeks. Trying and failing had become too discouraging.

"Maybe…," she started to say.

"But it doesn't do any good if I can't go into the halfworld anyway," I snapped, knowing what she was thinking.

"Don't shout at me," she said. "You *can* go into the halfworld. You did, and you took me and Blaze with you. You can do it again."

"I couldn't when those soldiers came along…And I've tried. I tried nearly every night, those first weeks we were in the Westwood."

"Maybe you were trying too hard. Maybe you should, I don't know, not *think* so hard. You know, when I'm trying to remember something I've forgotten, the harder I try, the more I can't remember it. But when I stop trying, it usually just comes back."

"That's not the same."

"It might be. What were you doing, the time it worked back at Cragfoot Lake?"

I shrugged.

"Well, you can't even try until it gets dark. There certainly aren't any deep shadows out here on the edge." Annot got to her feet and strung her bow. "I'm going to find us something to eat. What would you like?"

I tried to smile. "Pork pie?"

"The elusive mountain pork pie. I'll see what I can do. Don't go falling over the cliff. Come on, Blaze. We have to let the warlock think. Or figure out how not to think."

It was kind of her to give me that time alone. I found some shadow, where a twisted juniper grew close against the mountainside, and as soon as Annot was out of sight I stood there, in the darkest place between tree and rock, and tried to sink into it. I was there an hour at least, as the sun slowly crawled westwards. By the end I was nearly ready to cry from frustration.

I was supposed to be intelligent. Dame Hermengilde had thought so. The masters at Fowler College had thought so, although that hadn't stopped them letting Master Arvol steal Dame Hermengilde's money and make me a kitchen boy. Why couldn't I figure this out? I was supposed to be a Nightwalker, or half a Nightwalker. And I had done it before.

Worst of all, Annot thought I could do it.

And I had.

But always by accident.

So, I asked myself, what were you doing when it happened? Hiding.

Not beating at the darkness with my thoughts, trying to make it let me in. Only hiding. Only *being* shadow, being darkness, one with the shadows, one with the night.

And with that, I felt myself sinking, saw the world fade to gray.

The bridge was there as solid as the mountain, as stone always was in the halfworld.

I stood at the edge of the bridge, my heart pounding, my hands cold, my knees so weak I could hardly stay upright. I felt ahead with one foot. The stones of the bridge were there, solid and rough underfoot.

If the bridge dissolved beneath me, I did not want Annot to have to watch me fall.

I stepped out onto it and crossed, almost running. On the far side I let out a yell of pure joy, which echoed and re-echoed off the mountains.

I would have liked to rest a moment. My legs felt wobbly as jelly. I could see Annot, though, a gray ghost making her way down a steep, shale-covered slope, some small animal dangling from her hand, Blaze's leash tied to her waist.

"Mau—reeey!" she called, reaching the place she had left me. "Maurey?"

"I'm here!" I shouted.

"Maurey? Where are you? Maurey!"

"Annot, I'm over here. I've crossed the bridge!"

"Maurey! Where are you?"

She couldn't hear me. I didn't want to leave the halfworld, or even think about leaving it, not when we were on opposite sides of the gorge and especially not while I was on the bridge. When you try very hard not to sneeze, you know you will. But I could hear the panic in her voice; she would be thinking I had slipped and fallen over the cliff or something worse. I had to go back to her. I shut my eyes a moment, breathing deeply to calm myself. I was a shadow, a drifting darkness, that was all.

I walked back out onto the bridge.

Annot had stopped shouting. She was looking around, a hand over her mouth. I saw her creep up to the edge and peer over, as though half-expecting to see my body broken below. Then she went back and puzzled over the ground where I had stood between the juniper and the rock, looking at the pressed-down grass. Blaze sniffed the ground and wagged his tail, not very helpfully.

"Boo!" I shouted, jumping off the bridge, feeling myself slide back to the daylight world at the same time.

Annot screamed and threw the dead hare at me. She fell to her knees, and laughing, I dropped down and flung my arms around her. Annot was laughing too, a sort of gasping, choking laugh that is just about the same as screaming and crying.

"It's all right," I said, pulling her close as Blaze leapt around us, not certain what was going on but barking excitedly. "I did it, I went across the bridge. I think I've figured it out. Annot, it's all right." I shook her gently, and she thumped her fists on my chest.

"If you ever," she said, gasping between every word, "do that to me again, I'll...," and she burst into tears. "I thought you'd fallen, I thought you'd fallen."

"I called. Didn't you hear me?"

"No."

"It echoed off the mountains. I really shouted."

"I didn't hear anything." She wiped her eyes on my shirt and hit me one more time. "You are a beast."

"I'm sorry. I didn't think you'd...I just wanted to surprise you."

"You did that. I'm glad I wasn't standing on the edge of the damned cliff."

"Yes."

"Maurey?"

"What?"

"You can let go of me now."

"Sorry." I sat back on my heels. Annot stood up and dusted

herself off, rubbing her sleeve over her face, which just smudged it worse.

"It's your own fault," she said.

"What is?"

"Supper." Annot pointed. Blaze had pulled loose from his leash and was tearing hungrily into the hare.

✳ Chapter Nine ✳
The Ghosts

We crossed the bridge that night. I slipped into the halfworld again, pulling Annot and Blaze with me, and under night's shadow, we walked over stones that seemed solid and ancient as the mountains themselves.

Annot kept her eyes closed the whole time, and in the morning I found her grip on my hand had left bruises.

We camped on the highway on the far side of the bridge, and with dawn we went on, following the sharp bends of the road as it climbed higher and higher. No matter how high it climbed, though, the mountains were higher still. The Greyrock Pass seemed to twist between two great jagged peaks, clinging to the side of a broken valley. The river foamed and roared far below, and many smaller brooks went crashing down in long falls of spume and spray to join it. The trees were mostly juniper and larch and some sort of dwarf birch, and what flowers there were seemed to me to belong to an earlier season. Pink roses bloomed, their red stems hugging the ground, and we even found ripe strawberries. But it was cold, and every morning frost turned the world to a burning, glittering dream of ice. Every morning too, Annot woke looking bleak and haunted, truly haunted, because every night she dreamed of those who had died, trying to force their way through the pass to ravage Talverdin. But she always cheered up by the time breakfast was over, and I never saw the shades of the dead again, so I began to think I had been right, and the night-mares were only an enchantment meant to frighten humans into turning back.

We started early in the mornings and walked until nearly sunset, stopping frequently to rest. The air grows thinner the higher up one goes, and we felt like we were climbing an end-less stair. The highway twisted from side to side, following the twists of the mountainside, and dropped steeply up and down, though always rising overall. The muscles of our calves ached and cramped.

"Still," said Annot as we sat on a boulder to rest, on the third afternoon since crossing the bridge, "this isn't nearly as bad as I thought. I mean, there haven't really been any enchantments, other than the bridge and the bad dreams. In the ballads I've heard and the histories I've read, the pass is supposed to be quite terrible."

"It could get worse," I said.

"I think whatever spells guard this pass must recognize you. They're letting you through. You don't dream about dead knights."

"The bridge didn't let me through. I had to figure it out for myself."

"Well, if you hadn't been a warlock, we'd have spent days looking for a way to get down and cross the river, wouldn't we? You did figure it out, and we crossed safely."

The night before, I had dreamed that I lost my grip on Annot as we crossed, and that she fell, the bridge dissolving beneath her. I could still feel her hand sliding out of mine and hear Blaze's frantic barking as they dropped.

"I don't think we should get too confident," I said, digging my fingers into the deep warm fur of the dog's ruff, trying to drive away the horribly real feeling of the nightmare. "We're not out of the mountains yet."

"Gloomy fish," Annot said.

But I was right. We were not.

We trudged onwards. Even Blaze trudged, now, rather than prancing ahead as he had in the forest. Game was scarce in the mountains, and the trout were small, no longer than my hand. Many of the plants were new to Annot, so we didn't dare eat them. It took a lot of work to keep ourselves and Blaze fed, and we all felt tired and hungry most of the day.

"You know," Annot said as we walked, "I've decided something, Maurey."

"What?"

"I'd rather be a forest outlaw than a mountain bandit. I don't like mountains."

"I'd rather be a university master. Three meals a day and someone else to cook them."

"What about a baron? Would you like to be baron? You wouldn't have to do your own cooking then, either. Hah!"

A ptarmigan burst up out of the scrubby bushes by the roadside, wings whirring. Annot always carried her bow strung now, to take advantage of such moments. She whipped out an arrow, drew, took aim and shot.

The ptarmigan plummeted.

The road ahead bent sharply around a shoulder of rock, and it was behind this that the bird fell.

"Supper!" Annot cried gleefully and broke into a run. Keeping a tight hold on Blaze's leash to stop him getting to it first, I chased after her. There was a dizzying moment as I reached the projecting lump of rock, hard on her heels. I saw two highways, two smooth stretches of closely fitted stones, the blanket of moss and dry lichens creeping over them. One continued straight, hazy with mist, visible and then invisible, nothing but a stony slope overgrown with scrubby birch. The other bent around the rock and followed a flatter way. Except it did not. It went on, ghost-pale and insubstantial, out over a sudden ravine, while the paving stones themselves ended mere yards ahead of Annot's leaping run.

"I don't see it," she was calling. "It should have fallen on the road here."

"*Stop!*" I shouted. Screamed, really.

Annot froze and looked back over her shoulder. "What? Maurey, are you all right? You look sick."

I felt sick.

"Don't...move," I said. "There's...there's a cliff. Annot, there's a cliff."

"Where?"

"Right in front of you. Come back."

She stared at me. "What do you mean? I don't see any cliff. It just goes on."

"No! Come back."

Annot gave me a look. She ripped up a clump of moss from the road beneath her feet.

"I am on the road, right?"

"Yes, but it ends just in front of you. *Don't move!*"

Annot turned away and hurled the moss out ahead of her. I watched as it fell, breaking into several scattered pieces, down through the ghostly illusion of a road.

"Well," said Annot after a moment, "I think it certainly should have landed on the road by now, if it was going to." She sat down rather suddenly. "Where's the edge?"

"About…about a yard ahead of you."

"Huh. And where's my ptarmigan? And my arrow? It was a good arrow."

"Probably in the brook down there." I joined her, peering over the edge that only I could see. "Can't you hear the water?"

Annot listened. "I hear wind, in pine trees."

"There aren't any pine trees."

"True." She shut her eyes. "The noise is still trees. I mean, it still sounds like trees to me. Where's the edge?"

I took her hand and guided it to where the last of the real stones of the false highway ended, patted her palm over gravel, bent her fingers over the sudden dropping of the slope.

Annot went nearly as pale as I was. "So much for dinner," was all she said. "Poor ptarmigan, dying for nothing."

"Ravens," I said. "They'll find it."

There were ravens all through the mountains. Sometimes I thought they watched us.

And there were bones at the bottom of the slope. A round white skull, long bones, a horse's spine, rusted bits of metal that after a moment I could see were fragments of plate armor and mail. Then I saw another skull, and more bones, human and horse, more armor. I remembered a ballad about the most recent attempt to invade Talverdin. Some Eswyn knight had gathered a band of reckless young men and set out about fifty years before, never to be heard from again.

"This is as far as they got," I said aloud.

"Who?"

"Sir Willem Whitefax. You know, 'When will my Willem ride home, ride home, With his banners so gold in the morning…

His bones they lie bleaching on Talverdin's crags, And he'll never ride home in the morning.' Him. Or someone like him."

"That's horrible. You're right, though. I can hear water now."

"Can you see?"

"I can see…something. It's like looking at a reflection in water. It keeps shimmering, and I can still see the road. But," Annot said, squinting, "I can see the bottom too. Oh. There are bones down there. A lot of them."

"I know."

After a moment she said. "Maurey? You can go in front from now on."

"Yes."

I led the way back to where the real highway ran, through a shifting mist that was like the grayness of the halfworld, but torn and drifting, damp on the skin.

"So strange," muttered Annot, trying to walk with her eyes shut for a moment, holding on to my elbow. "All I can see is the rocks we should be tripping over and the trees we should be crashing through. And I can feel them catching at my clothes and my boots sliding. But when I shut my eyes, the road's there under my feet. Smooth."

"You're staggering like you're drunk, though," I said. "Maybe you should keep your eyes shut."

"It's trying to step on stones that aren't there," she said. "And all those invisible bushes." She let go of me and promptly tripped. "You just want me to hang onto you."

"Maybe," I said.

"Hah." Then she grabbed at me, stumbling again. "This is ridiculous. Blaze isn't tripping over illusions."

"Just hold my hand," I said. "I promise not to enjoy it."

"What's the point, then?" she asked and gave me a smile that made me stumble over my own feet.

That night I saw the ghosts again. We made camp under an overhang and stacked up loose stone to make a windbreak for our fire. The wind bit with the edge of winter and howled down the mountainside.

I heard voices. Men wept with despair and cursed the warlocks. Grown men cried for their mothers. "Lost," they cried, "lost forever in these accursed mountains."

Annot and I huddled together, wrapped in the blankets, sharing the heat of our bodies. Blaze, lying pressed against us, was like a big bearskin himself.

"Can you hear them?" I asked.

"Hear who?"

"The voices."

Annot gave me a worried look. "Just the wind."

So I knew these voices were no illusion meant to drive us back. An illusion should have affected Annot, not me. The voices were the shades of dead invaders, trapped here.

Annot fell asleep, curled into as tight a knot as Blaze. I could not sleep. The shades of the dead began to gather, thin, pale, half-seen figures.

"Let us go," begged one who wore a master's gown and hood. "Let us go home."

"You're dead," I whispered.

"But we want to go home, to rest in our own land, where Fescor can find us and lead us to Geneh. Why do you hold us here? Haven't we suffered long enough?"

"How long must we be punished?" cried another, a man who

looked like he could have ridden with King Hallow himself, the style of his mail hauberk was so antique. "How long until you forgive us? I only killed in battle. I never lit the philosopher's fire. I killed no children. Warlock, let me go."

"We are all guilty," snapped the master, "but warlock, let us go. Please. Must we be tormented, trapped in your spells, for eternity? Why?"

"Why are you haunting my friend's dreams?" I demanded, sounding rather braver than I felt. "She's never done anything to you. She's human."

"It is our task," the master said. "It is our doom. We warn others of the fate that will come to them if they attack Talverdin. But you are a Nightwalker and of powerful blood. You can release us. Haven't we served long enough? Surely no punishment should last for ever."

"Please," cried the knight, "please set us free. Be merciful, great prince."

"I'm not a great prince," I said. "And I don't know anything about these spells. I didn't trap you here. You trapped yourselves. Why couldn't you leave Talverdin alone? You already had the rest of their island." Our island, I told myself, but I didn't say it aloud. I still didn't feel like I belonged to Talverdin, not in my bones.

"You are a Nightwalker. You are a warlock and of royal blood. You could release us." The master clasped his hands together. "In Phaydos' name, bid us go free. Is this just? Is this right? You are a warlock, a prince, a powerful man, yes. But young and kind. Speak the words, let us go."

"Please," said the knight.

If it had been the knight alone asking, and if I had known what words would release him…but the vast crowd, pressing and whispering behind him with a noise like poplar leaves in the wind, was frightening simply in its mass, and the master...He reminded me of Chancellor Holden. His pleas did not come from his heart. He only saw a boy, someone he could control by intimidation and flattery, by making that boy feel guilt for something he had no part in creating. All he saw was a tool with the power to give him what he wanted.

Yet I did feel sorry, even for him.

"I want to go home," a boy's voice cried from the back of the throng. "Please, prince, be merciful. Let me go home."

I wrapped my arms around my head. "I can't," I said. "I don't know how. I don't know any magic. I'm not a warlock. I'm not a prince."

"Say the words," the shade of the master said. "Just say the words."

"What words?" I said. "I don't know any words. Leave me alone."

The ancient knight bowed, accepting what I had said. I felt as bad as if I had cursed a beggar.

"If we get to Talverdin," I said. "Sir Knight, if we get to Talverdin, I'll ask them if you can go. That's all I can promise."

The master sniffed and drifted away, but most of the shades began to whisper again, "He'll speak to the queen. He'll speak for us. He'll plead for us. A merciful Nightwalker."

"Thank you," the knight said and bowed again. "I always found your people honorable enemies, warlock."

They began to dissipate like a morning fog when the sun climbs above it.

In her sleep, Annot sighed, uncoiling a little, and her face relaxed. I wondered if she were having a pleasant dream for once, as I settled down back to back with her and pulled a fold of blanket up over my ear. It was so cold. I hoped the road would begin to descend the other side of the pass soon. We would freeze to death if we went much higher.

I had slept only a little when my own shivering woke me. Our fire had died nearly to embers, and the wind howled, sweeping in under our sheltering rock. I could not see more than my arm's length away—the razor-sharp wind was thick with snow.

Annot and Blaze were gone.

❊ CHAPTER TEN ❊
THE STORM AND THE TWINS

I stood up, peering into the darkness. I wasn't used to this. Everything was dark. The snow hid all the night colors I would normally have seen. The hollow beside me where Annot had lain was cold, but that was no indication of how long she had been gone; it would not have taken long for it to cool off. And the wind had filled with snow any tracks she might have left.

"Annot!" I shouted, but the wind snatched the words away. "Blaze?" I tried calling. "Blaze, boy, where are you?" Dogs have sharp hearing. I heard, faintly, an answering bark, upwind.

I wrapped myself in the blanket like a cloak and set out in that direction, pausing every few yards to shout again. Finally I heard Annot's voice as well as the dog's barking.

"Maurey?"

"Annot!"

"Where are you?"

"Here. Where are you?"

"Here!"

"Stay where you are. I'll come to you."

Another few yards and I found them. Annot had a bundle of sticks under her arm.

"There you are," she said. "I thought you were lost."

"Me!"

"I meant that I had lost you."

"What on earth did you go wandering off in the dark for? It's storming, or didn't you notice?"

"Well, it wasn't a few minutes ago. I woke up and it was cold. The fire was dying. So I thought I'd get more wood. It started to snow as soon as I got up, and then all of a sudden it was like this, a blizzard. Which way is the camp? I've gotten all turned around."

"This," I said, pointing. I hoped I was right. I'd never seen the world so dark. We started walking in the direction I thought I had come, but after a while Annot stopped.

"This isn't right," she said. "We should be back at our camp by now. And I think we're going downhill."

I changed my direction.

"No, wait," Annot said. "We'd better just make a new camp. We can find our supplies once the storm clears. The shepherds say the worst thing you can do when you're lost in a storm is to keep staggering around blindly."

Blind. That gave me an idea.

"Take my hand," I said. "Let's see what the halfworld looks like."

"You think this is an illusion?" Annot's teeth were chattering. So were mine. I could barely feel her hand grasping my own. "It certainly feels real."

I grasped Blaze's collar with my free hand, feeling some warmth seep into my fingers from him. We might be able to survive if we huddled up close with him. If the storm didn't go on too long. That was the wrong sort of thing to think, when I was trying to be calm, to be still. I took several deep breaths with my eyes shut and made myself part of the shadows, pulling Annot and the dog with me.

It was still snowing.

"At least I can see, now," I said. Not very far, it was true, but in the grayish light I could see the shape of the land a little, before the blowing snow obscured it all. "I think our camp's back that way."

Tripping over unseen stones and crashing through bushes, we found our way back to the overhanging rock. Our fire had died, and snow was already beginning to cover the charred remains. We scraped the snow away with our feet and tried to light a new fire, but the wind whipped the first timid flames away, and the snow quickly covered the wood and settled on the dry lichen in Annot's tinderbox, melting in the heat of her breath. Then the damp tinder wouldn't take a spark.

Annot tried. I tried. Our fingers were numb, freezing to the enameled box. I dropped it in the snow, my hands too stiff to grasp it properly. The snow covered our wood, covered us. I dug for the tinderbox and Annot shook out all the snow, tucked it inside her clothes against her shift. Given time, her body heat would dry the lichen, the flint and steel, and we could try again to start a fire. If we lived that long. We made the windbreak higher with the branches she had gathered and sat, wrapped in the blankets, with our backs against the rock. With Blaze curled up over our feet, we didn't feel too cold. But even Blaze's thick coat could not protect him forever. We held hands, not speaking. There was nothing to say.

Annot sighed and leaned her head on my shoulder. After a while I fell asleep too.

Voices woke me, speaking some incomprehensible language. I grunted and tried to turn away.

"I said, are you a human?"

It was a young woman's voice, but not Annot's. I didn't want to wake up. I was having such a good dream. I was in bed at home, at Dame Hermengilde's, with a blanket pulled up around my ears. But Master Arvol had crept into the room and opened the window, and the wind was blowing in. Dame Hermengilde would come and send him away. She would make everything right. I shut my eyes tighter and tried to slip back into my dream.

"Maybe he doesn't speak Eswyn human either. Try Ronish."

"The girl isn't Ronish. She's Eswyn for certain."

"Dunmorran. They call themselves Dunmorran in the northern kingdom now."

"Eswy, Dunmorra, they're all the same."

It sounded to me like one voice arguing with itself. A voice that had forgotten it was still speaking a language we could understand.

"They'll die here, whatever they are."

"It surprises me they're not dead already. How did they even cross the bridge?"

"He's not human."

"We could put a sleeping spell on them, get the horses and take them back to the human side of the bridge."

"Stopping the snow would be easier. But would they have the sense to go back to Greyrock?"

"Probably not, if they haven't given up before now. And where are the ghosts?"

"Sulking about something. I think we should take these two up to the guardhouse. Because *he* is not fully human. Someone will want to see him."

"She *is* a human."

"Well, you can carry her back to the human side of the border, then. Unless you really want to leave her here to die."

A sigh. "They're just children."

I tried to make an indignant noise.

"He's awake, I think. Are you awake, boy?" Someone shook me roughly by the shoulder.

"Errr," I said, or something like that, trying to force my eyes open.

The snow was falling more gently than it had, and it was gray morning. A face swam before me, blurry in the snow. One face, two faces, face and reflection. They were white-skinned, black-eyed, and bundled up in dark cloaks so that there wasn't much else to see.

"Wake up," said one. "You'll freeze to death."

There was something important I had to remember...

"Annot!"

She was still beside me. Ignoring the warlocks, I shook her, and when she didn't move, shook her again, hard enough to rattle her teeth.

"What?" she mumbled, sliding down onto my lap.

"Eswyn humans, I said, and I was right," remarked one of the identical faces, rather smugly. She pulled Annot back up. "Come, human. Wake up."

"Maurey?" Annot asked, opening her eyes. "Maurey, it's cold. Where's Blaze?"

Hearing his name, Blaze thrust his head between the two young Nightwalkers and huffed anxiously in Annot's face. He didn't seem to mind the two warlocks, and that gave me a little hope. But perhaps they had some spell for making animals friendly.

"Maurey?" said one of the young women.

"*Maurey?*" said the other, like an echo. Then she said something more, in a language I didn't understand, although it seemed to be addressed to me.

I shook my head.

The two conferred quickly.

"Maurey," said one of them. "Your name is *Maurey?*"

"Yes," I said.

"Hah. *I* said you were not human. *She* said you were not Talverdine—Nightwalker. You bear the blood of both, yes?"

"I guess so." But I could hardly get the words out, my teeth chattered so.

"Come along," said the other Nightwalker. "Annot, are you called, child? Can you stand?"

With the aid of one of the women, Annot managed to get to her feet. I forced myself up and stood swaying.

"Annot," said the Nightwalker woman, patting her on the back. "That's right. Come on. Not far now."

"Oh," said Annot vaguely. "Good." She touched Blaze's head for comfort. He stood with his shoulder against her leg, as though he tried to help hold her up. "I'm not," she added, "a child."

The other Nightwalker offered me her arm, like a gentleman escorting a lady onto a dance floor. I took it, and we staggered off.

"My name is Jessmyn," the young woman said. "And my sister is Aljess. You may not have noticed, but we're twins."

"Oh," I said.

"Too tired for humor?" Jessmyn asked. "Well, that's what happens when you sleep in the snow."

"We couldn't get the fire going," I said.

"Yes." Jessmyn hesitated. "The storm is meant to happen if humans come this far along the pass. It hasn't been—what is the phrase…set off?—yes, the guardian storm hasn't been set off in over a hundred years. We hoped whoever had set it off would turn back, but we also knew that humans are not very sensible, so finally we decided it was time to look for frozen humans."

"And we found some!" Aljess called back.

"A human and a half. And a dog."

I wasn't sure I liked being called half a human, even though it sounded like a joke. It was almost worse than "just children."

But they seemed quite cheerful and friendly, and they could have left us to die.

"Do you live near here?" I asked, trying to be friendly in my turn.

"Live? No. We're taking our turn as border guards this month, manning the watchtower at the high point of the pass. Very boring."

"Guards?"

I almost said, but you're girls.

"All the knights take a turn," she said.

"Are you—old enough to be knights?" I asked. For all their talk of us as children, I didn't think they were really more than a couple of years older than we were. Jessmyn snorted.

"Are you old enough to be invading Talverdin?"

"We weren't—!" But I realized she was teasing again.

"Why were you trying to cross the pass?"

"It seemed like a good idea at the time," I mumbled. "Chancellor Holden wants to kill me."

Jessmyn hissed at the name. "Holden," she said flatly. "Maynar damn him. I imagine he does. That's a man who'd burn a brown-eyed baby if he thought he could get away with it, just in case it had a Nightwalker great-grandpapa. Not surprising that he wanted to burn you, with that handsome face. And you couldn't leave your sweetheart behind? That's very touching, but you very nearly got her killed."

"She's not..." I felt myself blushing, hoping Annot hadn't heard and half-hoping she had. "Anyway, it was all her idea. They would have burned me if she hadn't rescued me. Holden probably wants to kill her now too. Neither of us can go back."

"We have to see your king," said Annot.

"I imagine you do," Aljess said. "Although it's the queen you must see. Our last king died, oh, twelve years ago now, Genehar keep him. His daughter Ancrena rules now."

Maynar and Genehar, I was thinking. We were taught that the Nightwalkers denied the Seven Powers and worshipped demons of chaos, but Maynar and Genehar were names found on ancient monuments from the days of Good King Hallow; they were merely older forms of Mayn, Queen of Night, and Gench, Lady of Birth and Death. Or were those carved stones older than Hallow's day? I know one of the masters at the college claimed so, though Master Holden had forbidden him to teach it.

"We have to see her right away," Annot said. "Chancellor Holden's going to come here with an army. He has Maurey's ring, and he thinks it's some sort of key to let him through the Greyrock Pass. He's cutting a new road through the Westwood for the army. They were hiring men in the forest to work clearing the road this autumn. Next summer, maybe even the spring, that's how soon they'll come. At least that's what a soldier told me."

Aljess and Jessmyn had another hurried conversation in the Nightwalker language, Talverdine, as I later found out it was called. It used to be called Eswian, when the warlocks ruled all the island of Eswiland. But now a word nearly the same as that name, Eswyn, meant the language I had grown up speaking, the tongue of the human kingdoms of Dunmorra and Eswy. No wonder the grammar-school pupils sometimes find history so confusing.

"You will see the queen," said Jessmyn.

"She will want to see you, I think," Aljess agreed, "as quickly as possible, as you say. A road built and a key to the Greyrock Pass found. This is not good news."

We left the highway and climbed straight up the mountainside on a narrow path I don't think I would ever have noticed, even had it not been covered with snow. The higher we climbed, the less snow there was, until we were walking on dry stones and green plants again. We passed a mountain buttercup, bright with white bloom, and a thicket of blackberry vines with fruit only beginning to ripen. Already the air was noticeably warmer, and my hands and feet began to ache with the beat of my heart, as feeling returned.

The gray stone watchtower blended in with the mountainside. Lichen covered it, and gnarled pines clustered by its door. The tower was well-placed to overlook this highest point of the pass. Gazing down, I could see the highway below, winding back east towards Greyrock, west to Talverdin. Or at least, I could see the blinding swirl of snow that covered it.

"Now," said Jessmyn, "the first thing we do is we thaw you out."

"The first thing we do," said Aljess, "is we stop the snow."

"You stop the snow. I'll thaw our guests."

They ushered us through the door into what seemed to be a stable. Two moon-white horses with blue-gray muzzles and ears regarded us over the doors of their stalls. A huge fawn-and-black tabby cat arched his back, hissed at Blaze and leaped to the safety of a beam.

"This is Grig," Aljess said, as though introducing us to the queen herself, "the Warden of the Tower."

We stared. I had heard so many stories of the dark powers of the warlocks that it seemed perfectly possible the commander of this tiny garrison could be a shapeshifter. Annot later confessed she had the same thought.

Aljess looked at our faces and hooted with laughter. "No, no," she said, patting my shoulder. "He's supposed to keep the mice out of our supplies. But you know what cats are like. He acts as though he's lord of the place, and we poor knights who come and go are his humble guests."

My ears grew hot, but that might have been from coming in out of the biting wind.

We climbed a flight of stone stairs that wound around the walls to a second-story room where a fire still roared on the hearth.

"Sit down," ordered Jessmyn. "Take your boots off. I'll find warm socks."

"Blankets," said Aljess. "Hot drinks."

"And the book. You need the book to stop the snow, or now that it has gathered strength, it will go on as long as Annot is here or until the clouds run out of moisture."

Annot and I were hustled into chairs, bundled into soft blankets, our sweaty socks stripped off and ones belonging to the twins pulled on. A pot of soup, thick with beef, barley, and kale, and a pitcher of watered, honeyed wine were fetched from the larder and set to warm on the hearth.

Jessmyn treated us like babies, tipping cups of mulled wine to our lips, spooning the soup, but I was glad she did. I could hardly bend my fingers, and how they burned when I tried.

"Not very bad," Jessmyn said, checking our hands and turning our faces this way and that, looking for signs of frozen flesh. "You could be far worse. You were fortunate it's only late summer and the storm had to work very hard against nature even to be as cold as it was."

"It felt cold enough," I said.

"But you only have a little frostbite and nothing worse. Come with me. We'll carry your friend to bed, and then you can tell me how you came to be here. I must send a raven with a message to the court to ask what to do with you, but I need to know your story first."

Jessmyn and I carried Annot to a bed in the next room and tucked her in, with Blaze lying across her feet.

Back in the sitting room, Aljess was muttering over a dark, old-looking book, holding a handful of night-black hair out of her face with one hand, propping her chin up on the other. She looked up at my staring and smiled.

"It's a simple spell," she said. "So they say. Let's hope I don't turn the snow into a hailstorm, eh?"

"Or a rain of toads," murmured Jessmyn, and Aljess crossed her eyes at her sister.

They did not seem much like knights of any sort, except that they were both wearing trousers and knee-length tunics with leather jerkins over them, a bit like old-fashioned Gehtalandish costume, and they wore daggers in their belts. But I had been staring not so much at that, as at another face so like my own.

Or a pair of them.

"So tell me, Maurey," Jessmyn said, steering me back to my seat by the fire and passing me another cup of sweet spicy wine, which I found I could now wrap my fingers around. "Who are your parents? Why have you come to Talverdin only now? And what about this army?"

Aljess muttered something and thumped the book shut.

"Let it snow," she said. "I can do this later. I want to hear the story."

Once the twin knights had heard my tale, Aljess locked herself in an upper room of the tower to perform the spell that stopped the snow, and Jessmyn went to the roof, whistling. I followed her, although I was so tired I could hardly keep my eyes open.

When she saw I had followed, she gave me a wicked grin and said, "Hold out your hand, Maurey."

I did, and she slapped a chunk of raw greasy bacon into it, continuing to whistle, not a tune, now, but a sharp insistent note. With a swooshing murmur of wings, a glossy black raven plummeted from the sky to her arm. It cocked its head and examined the bacon in my hand suspiciously, first from one gleaming eye, then the other. Jessmyn stroked the back of its neck gently, bent her head close to it and began to murmur in musical-sounding Talverdine. When she straightened up, the raven shook itself and gave a harsh call that sounded like "Cra-aa-aark!" It snatched the bacon from my fingers and gulped it down before it launched itself into the air, disappearing into the distance.

"Now we wait," Jessmyn said, with a brilliant smile. "As the raven flies, it's not far to the castle that guards the end of the pass, what would be called in your tongue the Valley of Weeping." She must have seen my look of interest at the odd name, because she went on. "The valley is where the rear guard of our retreat halted to work the spells that sealed the mountains against humans and cut us off from our Eswiland. A place of sorrowful memories, you see. My commander there will no doubt send a raven on to the queen at Sennamor with his own message, but even so I expect we'll have our answer before too long."

"How?" I asked, stifling a yawn. "I'm sorry. But how do the ravens carry messages?"

Jessmyn laughed. "Warlock magic," she whispered, in what was probably meant to be an eerie and ominous voice. "A spell on them enables them to repeat the words they have been given."

I nodded, but my only other answer was a yawn too great to be hidden. The Nightwalker knight laughed at me again and with a hand on my shoulder, marched me back down and tucked me into the upper bunk of the two-tiered bed.

I slept that day right through, and the night, waking the following morning to find Annot and Aljess frying sausages while Jessmyn toasted slices of bread on a fork.

No raven had returned from either the commander of the Weeping Valley castle or from the queen, but late that evening, while Jessmyn and Aljess were trying to teach Annot and me some complicated game like chess with completely different pieces and moves, Aljess looked up.

"Is that the glass starting?" she asked.

"I think so." Jessmyn got up and crossed the room to the window. A lump of misshapen bluish glass sat on the sill, the sort of thing one might use as a paperweight, although it was so large and heavy it took both hands to hold it. She set it on the table. It seemed to be humming a single high, sweet note, which stopped as soon as Jessmyn murmured a word and passed her hand over its surface.

"What is it?" Annot asked.

"A watch-glass. It sees the pass, or a section of the pass, from the bridge up to this watchtower and halfway down towards the Valley of Weeping, where the highway descends from the mountains. In the past it saw the whole of the Greyrock Pass, of course, not just this highest section."

"Did it see us?"

"Well..." Aljess seemed reluctant to answer.

"Yes," admitted Jessmyn.

"It is small. We could not see that Maurey was one of us. There are many dark-haired humans, after all."

"So you were watching us, after we crossed the bridge," Annot said.

Aljess nodded.

"And you knew we were down there when the storm started. You weren't just guessing that there were humans trapped in the snow. Why didn't you help us sooner?"

"We are not here to help you. We are here to stop humans coming to Talverdin and killing us all," said Jessmyn. Then she shrugged.

"How does it work?" I asked. There was no point in blaming them for not rescuing us sooner—if we were rescued and not prisoners. I liked the twins, but they were knights of Talverdin, and Annot was human, I was half-human. I was not ready to call them friends yet.

"Magic," said Aljess. "The stone of the pass is transformed into glass. It...remembers being the pass. It knows what the stones know." She laughed. "I've been studying to become a Maker, but I still do not really understand how it works."

"A Maker?" I asked.

"A magician, you would say. A warlock." She gave a crooked smile. "I know you humans think we're all warlocks, but really, hardly anyone has the talent any more. You saw Jessmyn send a raven with a message, did you not? Well, anyone who knows the proper words may wake the memory spell the message-ravens carry. Anyone who knows the right words may see what the watch-glass shows. But to set the spells on the ravens, and to make such a thing as the watch-glass…there are few left who are capable of such arts. In the old days, the Makers would hardly have thought it worthwhile to train someone with as little talent as I have. But now—I'm not one of the best, but I am quite good, compared to some of the others. Still, I would rather be a knight than a Maker."

I stared. Someone who admitted she could do magic, not the philosophers' secret knowledge that some people called magic, but real, Nightwalker magic, and she wasn't truly interested in it.

"It's Elwinn, I think," Jessmyn said, drawing our attention back to the glass. She hunched over it, peering into its heart. "Elwinn and Sanno. They weren't due to relieve us for another week. I think we must be going back to the castle with you two. They have extra horses with them."

Some hours later, when Elwinn and Sanno arrived, that turned out to be the case. The two young men grumbled a bit about being sent up to the watchtower early, but it was very good-humored grumbling, and they seemed eager to see us, especially me.

I would have thought Annot would be the curiosity, being human. But Elwinn and Sanno spoke Eswyn just as well as Aljess and Jessmyn, and I began to suspect that Nightwalkers, or at least their adventurous young knights, traveled east of the mountains rather more than anyone in Dunmorra or Eswy suspected.

The message Elwinn and Sanno brought was that the Queen of Talverdin herself wanted to see Annot and me, without delay.

✳ Chapter Eleven ✳
The Queen of Talverdin

Our journey down the western side of the Greyrock Pass was nothing like our struggle up the eastern. The air was warm, birds sang, and the air was so clear that for one brief moment, between folds of the mountains, I had a glimpse of the distant gray-green sea. Talverdin's coast was as deadly as its mountains. The rocks, it was said, moved to crush invading ships. But from the mountainside it was serene and beautiful. For a moment I imagined what it would be like to be sailing out there, flying before the wind, leaving Holden and his hatred so far behind I could forget him forever.

"How far is it to the castle?" Annot asked.

"To the royal castle, Sennamor, you mean? About a day's easy riding, once we leave the mountains," Aljess answered.

"And the riding had better be easy," Jessmyn added. "Or we'll lose young Maurey."

"I could walk," I said.

"No, you could not," said Jessmyn. "It's you the queen wants to see, not us and not even Annot. Keep your heels down. Sit straight, you'll balance better."

"I have ridden before," I said with all the dignity I could muster.

"A very long time ago, I imagine," said Aljess.

"It's all right as long as she walks."

The white mare flicked a black ear back as if she had understood.

Jessmyn snickered. "We're not going to walk the horses all the way to Sennamor."

"You're doing well, really, Maurey," Annot said, "for someone who's out of practice."

In truth all the riding I had done had been with Harl Steward on his old mare. I had already fallen off this rather more lively mount twice and had once had to be rescued by Jessmyn, when the horse turned aside from the highway to graze. We had only left the watchtower that morning, the second day since our arrival, and already we had been riding too long, in my opinion. I was starting to hurt in all sorts of embarrassing places.

I hurt in even more by the time we reached the western end of the Greyrock Pass in what I thought of as Weeping Valley, late that afternoon. The valley was a narrow place, overlooked by a grim gray castle, the last defence against invasion if the spells on the pass failed. The commander, an elderly knight, rode out to speak with Jessmyn and Aljess. He and the men and women with him gave Annot and me many long thoughtful looks but did not speak to us. Nor were we invited back to spend the night. Bad enough that we had seen all the enchantments on the pass and knew where the watchtower was, I suppose. No need to show potential enemies and spies over the fortress as well. We spent the night camped in a gloomy spruce wood instead and made an early start the next morning.

Talverdin was a beautiful land. Between the low forested hills, the valleys curled, green with meadows, golden with ripening grain. The village houses were mostly long low buildings of gray stone with thatched or slate-shingled roofs. Gold-colored cattle with black-tipped horns grazed in the hillside pastures alongside spotted goats and black-faced sheep with curling horns and herds of the famous moon-white horses. In the orchards, the green plums and swelling apples bowed the branches. People came to the roadside to watch us ride past. It was strange to see people who looked so much like myself. Strange how different each face was from the one beside it.

Nightwalkers weren't supposed to be people. They were stories to make bad children behave. These people wore bright colored clothes and all of them, men and women both, wore their hair long, to the shoulders if not to the waist. The men wore short beards, and the women and girls, nearly all of them, braided flowers into their hair. I scratched at my itching chin, which was finally needing to be shaved (I hoped) and wondered how I would look in a beard, and if Annot would like it. After weeks in the woods, my hair was nearly to my shoulders anyway. The onlookers said little, just watched solemnly. Even those dressed most plainly looked like prosperous free peasants, content and confident. One or two nodded a cautious greeting when I met their eyes, and one little girl, held in her father's arms, pointed at Annot and waved. Some of the older girls, the ones about our age, stared openly at Annot's red-gold hair, putting their heads together and whispering as she rode past. Annot kept a pleasant smile fixed on her face. I imagined it was starting to hurt.

But human villagers, seeing real Nightwalkers riding down their dusty street in company with royal knights, would not have merely watched in quiet curiosity. They would have muttered and shouted insults. Someone would probably have begun throwing wormy windfall apples, if the knights did not move to prevent it.

But of course, we *were* riding with two of the queen's knights, and to make this clear the twins wore long hauberks of old-fashioned chain mail—it seemed as though Nightwalker weapons and armor had changed little since they retreated beyond the Greyrock Pass—with deep red surcoats over them, the royal oak leaf stitched in gold on the front and back. We were under royal protection. Still—there was no muttering that sounded angry, and few looked either frightened or resentful, though some were wary, and the little children hung back behind their parents' legs.

"This is what it was like for you at the college," Annot said quietly, "all the time. Oh, Maurey."

"A little," I admitted. "But no one's beating us. They're just looking, and you can't blame them. Most of them have probably never seen humans before."

"One human," Annot corrected.

I shrugged and considered a moment. "I think they like your hair; that's why they're whispering."

"It's red," Annot said in disgust. "They're probably wondering what's wrong with me and if it's catching."

"*I* like your hair," I said and turned red myself when she looked at me.

Aljess snorted and Jessmyn coughed behind her hand.

We traveled very slowly, mostly because I was such a poor rider, and reached the castle of the Queen of Talverdin late that next evening, when the setting sun was painting Sennamor's gray stone with copper light. I had expected a crowded little city, like Cragroyal, but we learned the only city in Talverdin was Dralla, away on the coast. Here, only a small market town lay at the castle's foot. People gathered to watch us ride past. I was surprised to see a woman blacksmith, setting down her hammer to step outside her forge, shading her eyes against the sun to stare at us. Jessmyn must have known her, for she waved. After a moment the woman smiled and waved back.

The gates of the castle opened for us, and we rode in through a long vaulted tunnel, which emerged into a grassy bailey, shadowy now with approaching dusk. Servants—boys and girls in stable smocks, who nudged one another, more interested in staring at me, it seemed, than at Annot—ran out to take the horses. A grander servant, a woman wearing a black robe with a gold chain looped across her chest, opened a door and gestured us into the central keep.

In silence we followed her up a broad flight of stone stairs to a hall rather like King Dugald's Hall of Judgement. The walls of the long room and of the staircase were hung with woven tapestries and embroidered hangings depicting men and women riding out in armor, fighting fabulous beasts like dragons and basilisks and lions, men and women sailing on ships with unicorn figureheads, men and women playing musical instruments in gardens so entangled with bright woven flowers that you could almost smell their perfumes. And all the men and all the women had skin as white as milk, and hair and eyes as black as the night sky.

It unsettled me. All over again, it didn't seem natural that the woven and embroidered people should look like me.

The woman with the gold chain, a steward, maybe, or a councillor, bowed to the figure on the throne at the far end of the hall. We all bowed too and followed her on. Under a canopy of brocade, a scene of unicorns and phoenixes, was a dais on which stood the throne, a plain chair of dark wood, but heavy, old and solid. The steward, if that is what she was, spoke in Talverdine to the woman seated on the throne, before stepping back to take a seat on the cushioned bench along the wall.

Quite a number of people sat there quietly waiting in the shadows, watching, and more stood in little groups. Their eyes gleamed, and the patterns embroidered on their long formal robes, mostly birds and flowers and fantastic beasts, shimmered and shifted in the breeze, glowing with their own velvet-dark night colors.

There were no candles. The only light came from a few high narrow windows, the last of the twilight leaking in to give the shifting night hues of the tapestries and robes, and the water-swirl night color of the stone floor, a reddish cast. Annot felt for my hand, and I realized she could hardly see at all. Her fingers were cold. I squeezed her hand.

The woman sitting on the throne, the queen, spoke to Jessmyn and Aljess, and they answered. They didn't seem frightened, or apologetic, so I supposed they were not being told it was all a dreadful mistake and they should have left us to freeze to death. Then the queen held out a hand.

"Maurey," she said, "come here. Let me look at you."

She had more of an accent than either of the twins or the two knights who had replaced them on duty at the watchtower. I stepped forward reluctantly. Annot's grip on my hand tightened and she followed, clinging close. Blaze shook his ears mightily and padded after us.

The hall was as silent as the lifeless crypts beneath the colleges. I stopped after I had gone only a few paces. No guards stood by the throne, but I realized that men and women in mail shirts, with swords and spears, were scattered through the little knots of people in court robes, and one or two nearby had shifted as if our moving closer to the queen made them uneasy.

"Let the woman and the dog stay there," the queen said. "Maurey, come." She pointed right to the edge of the dais.

I swallowed, noticing for the first time that though she was wearing a long robe of the darkest purple, with golden oak leaves and acorns and silver unicorns twining around its hems and up around the neck, shimmering in the near-darkness, she held a sheathed sword on her lap.

Annot took a deep breath and let go my arm. "At least she didn't call me a child," she muttered, but in the silent hall her voice carried farther than she intended, and someone tittered. The queen's face remained expressionless, and Annot blushed, pushing me away.

I went on. One of the twin knights, I wasn't sure without looking back if it was Jessmyn or Aljess, came to stand beside Annot.

"Your Grace," I said, stopping at the edge of the platform. My voice trembled a little. I bowed, not sure what else to do. I had a sudden vision of her drawing that heavy blade and sweeping my head from my shoulders.

The queen looked at me, that was all, but I could feel her eyes traveling over my face, hot and burning as the beams of the sun.

She was older than the king of Dunmorra—my brother Dugald, that was still a strange thought to me—perhaps nearing forty, I judged. Her hair was sleek and black and reached to her waist, and she wore a circlet of gold with a single square red stone set in the center, like a fiery third eye in the middle of her forehead. She was not beautiful in the dainty way so much admired in Dunmorran women like Annot (who proved that dainty was not the same as fragile). Queen Ancrena had a strong angular face and a nose I would have called sharp, if I did not have an uneasy feeling that mine was sharper.

The queen continued to study me as though I were some poem to be committed to memory in order to avoid a beating from the schoolmasters.

"Tell me about yourself, Maurey," she said at last.

"What—what do you want to know, Your Grace?" I stammered.

"Everything," she said. "Start with where you were born and when. Finish with how you came to be where Jessmyn and Aljess found you." I noticed she did not say "captured," which was hopeful. "And tell me everything you can about Chancellor Holden's plans and how you learned of them."

Of course, that would be why the whole court was gathered: Jessmyn had sent that raven with a message, and now they would want to know the details of the threat from Holden. I felt a little relieved, as though all the watching eyes were not so much on me in person anymore. It was Chancellor Holden, the road he was making through the Westwood to Greyrock Pass and the army he intended to lead along it next spring that concerned them.

But I began at the beginning, as the queen instructed. She listened intently, sitting up straight, tapping her fingers on the jewelled scabbard of her sword and sometimes frowning a little.

Some parts of my story evoked whispers and angry-sounding muttering in quiet Talverdine. The queen herself shook her head sympathetically when I told of Dame Hermengilde's death and how I had found myself overnight turned from a young gentleman to not much more than a slave, and smiled at Annot when I described how she and Blaze had invaded the Hall of Judgement, driving the herd of swine before them. One of the twins laughed aloud. But they were all silent when I described the meeting with the company of royal men-at-arms and their task: to find a route for a road to be cleared on which an army could march. The queen made me describe too, in careful detail, the second of the rings Chancellor Holden had taken from me; the one he did not give to the king. And it seemed to me the whole court held its breath while I did so.

And as I had promised the shade of the ancient knight of King Hallow's army, I asked—my voice shaking again, since I knew it was futile and presumptuous—if they would release the human ghosts from their bondage.

"I promised," I faltered. "I told them I would ask."

"You have asked," the queen said. "We will not free them while the human kingdoms stand against us. They know this." And that, so far as Queen Ancrena was concerned, was clearly the end of the matter.

"Maurey, why did you come here? Tell me this."

"It was Annot's idea." They all turned their gaze to her. "She thought...we had to escape Holden. There was nowhere else we could go where he would not follow us. And Annot thought I would be safe here. She knew...she knew I was one of you before I would admit it myself."

"Only a half-breed," a man said.

I couldn't help but look back over my shoulder to find the speaker. He was one of those in embroidered robes sitting on the cushioned benches that lined the wall. An old man, his hair was streaked with silver, and his nearly white beard did not hide a jutting chin. His face seemed all sharp lines, as though a lifetime of disdain for all around him had dragged his face into a permanent sneer. When he saw me looking he smiled, the way that bully Calmic might have when he saw he had hurt someone.

The old man's smile vanished when the queen said something harsh in Talverdine. He rose to his feet and bowed, sitting down again without expression. I looked away. His eyes were narrowed, angry.

"Baroness Oakhold," the queen said then. "Did you take no thought for your own safety in electing to accompany your friend? My people and yours are enemies of long standing."

"I was afraid, Your Grace," said Annot. "But I couldn't let him go alone. He was only a little boy when he left Dame Hermengilde's manor at Erford for the city, and he hadn't been out of Cragroyal since. He would never have made it on his own—he knew nothing about how to live off the land. And I knew...I hoped, that you were a people of honor, that you would not treat me as an enemy once you knew I came intending you no harm."

"Unlike your own people?" the queen asked.

Annot scowled. "Yes," she said, "unlike we Dunmorrans and Eswyn, who treat anyone with black eyes and white skin like a monster. But remember too, Your Grace, Maurey's Dame Hermengilde and Harl Steward and Hanna Stewardswife. We're not all like Chancellor Holden and Master Arvol."

"There are rather more Holdens and Arvols, Baroness," the queen said dryly.

"But in time there could be more Dame Hermengildes," Annot said.

"And Baronesses Oakhold?"

"Why not? If we stopped teaching children to see warl...to see your people as evil, as monsters, if they learned to look on you just as people, no more strange than Ronishmen or the Fenlanders away in the north…"

"Yes, well," the queen said. "Perhaps. Some day. When we are all dead, your grandchildren will say, 'They were not so bad. Is it not a great pity they are gone?'"

She switched to Talverdine and seemed to be addressing the hall. All I could understand was Annot's name.

"I have told them you have the freedom of the land, Baroness Oakhold," the queen said then to her. "You have proven yourself a friend to Maurey, and by bringing us warning of Holden's plans, to all of Talverdin. You may come and go as you will, saving only that you may not enter the mountains or depart from the country without my leave, and you may not carry weapons in the royal presence."

Annot bowed and murmured her thanks. Even worried as I was, I realized what an honor it was that the queen would show a human such trust.

"And Maurey," the queen said.

"Your Grace?"

"What am I to do with you?"

"Your Grace?"

"You realize you are almost certainly my nephew?"

"I…oh."

I felt like an idiot. First not understanding that if the runaway Queen Rhodora of Dunmorra was my mother, then King Dugald must be my brother, and now this. It had been fixed for so long in my mind that I was a foundling, an orphan with no family at all—I could not seem to think of myself as having real, living relatives.

"I…I hadn't really thought about it, Your Grace. He…I…I

mean, I don't even know his name. My father's. Um, or, really, my mother's, except because of the rings, like I said, they said the rings were hers. Queen Rhodora's, I mean. Or one of them was."

"There is the ring," the queen said gravely. "But there is also your name. Maurey. My father the late king, Genehar give him rest, was Havlamaurey. And you look like him, a little. Like your grandfather. Mostly, though, you look like my brother, Prince Lishon." Ancrena smiled, sadly, it seemed to me. "No, I have no doubts at all, now that I see you and hear your story in full. You are my nephew. Poor Lishon. My father sent him to King Burrage's peace talks so that he could learn something of the human kingdoms and human ways. I was the eldest and the heir; I could not be risked." She sighed. "And there Lishon met Rhodora, a lonely young woman wed to an old man. I can understand their passion and pity it. I cannot forgive their irresponsibility. Between them, Lishon and Rhodora destroyed the best chance for peace between our peoples that has come about since Conqueror Hallow's day."

"I'm sorry, Your Grace."

Ancrena blinked at me. "Sorry? My poor Maurey, it is none of your doing. You are utterly blameless. And for what little time we have left, you have a home among us."

She spoke a little more in Talverdine, and a murmuring rose among the watchers. I had been wrong after all. It was as much myself as the news of Chancellor Holden's army that interested them. A lost prince? That was a strange, prickling thought. It made me feel like someone else entirely, like my skin did not fit me anymore. But the queen's words worried me.

"What do you mean, Your Grace?" I asked. "'What little time?' Holden isn't likely to come before next spring or summer, even if he's already started clearing the road. Can't the spells be changed by then, to prevent him, even if that ring is some sort of key to let him through the enchantments? *Is* that what the ring is?"

"In a way," the queen said. "That ring, Maurey, that Chancellor Holden took from you, the golden ring with the red stone carved with an oak leaf, is one of the great treasures of Talverdin. It is over four hundred years old. My father entrusted it to Prince Lishon, to give safe-conduct to a return embassy, if King Burrage proved to be sincere in his desire for peaceful relations. It was made with many spells to permit the passage of humans through the defences of the Greyrock Pass; we always had some friends among your people in the first few generations after Hallow's conquest. Humans had lived at peace among us, not slaves, not serfs, though your histories rarely admit that, long before Hallow came. Like us they were driven from their lands, to the fringes and the wild places, the forest and the fens. Not all contacts were severed, and we made more than a few such tokens. But this ring is a powerful one, capable of granting passage to a large party. It would have allowed Burrage to send an ambassador and his retinue to visit us, if the peace talks had gone well."

"Or an army," I said. "I do understand that, Your Grace."

"Yes, Maurey, the ring is a key. With the ring in his possession, Chancellor Holden can bring an army through the pass. The ghosts will not trouble them, the road will not shift, the rocks will not fall, the storms will leave them in peace. And the great halfworld bridge will be there for them, solid underfoot, unless we send war-locks, Makers as we call them, to throw it down before his army can come. Which we must do. That bridge took the labor of two generations to build, and we cannot make its like again."

"Why not, Your Grace?" It was Annot who asked that. "Why

can't you change the spells, like Maurey said, and make new ones that the ring can't prevent? Why haven't you done that already? You've had *years* since you knew the ring was lost in Dunmorra somewhere. Surely you must have prepared?"

Angry whisperings rose behind us. Annot raised her chin and ignored them.

The queen shook her head. "Such great spells are beyond us these days, Baroness. We do not know why. Our magic has dwindled since we were caged in Talverdin. In every generation, fewer children are born with the talent to be Makers, and none are as powerful or skilled as their parents or grandparents were. We cannot alter the spells that guard the Greyrock Pass. We cannot replace them with new, not on anything near the scale of the old."

Aljess had hinted at the weakening of magic when she tried to explain how the watch-glass worked, but I hadn't really thought about what that meant for Talverdin. The whisperings in the great hall were sharp with shock. That the queen should admit the Nightwalker kingdom's weakness to a human must have seemed incredible trust, or incredible foolishness.

Maybe Ancrena had so little hope that it did not matter to her anymore.

Annot bowed in the direction of the throne. "Your Grace," she said. "I...I am honored you place such trust in me." She hesitated. "I will do everything within my power to help defend your land. I'm...I'm very good with a bow."

That was treason to Dugald, her own king, and she knew it. The onlookers murmured again. I think she surprised them. "But," Annot went on, "I beg your pardon, Your Grace, but I notice no one is saying, '*King Dugald* can bring an army...' We all know it's Chancellor Holden we have to fear."

"We?" someone asked. "Little human, I do not think..."

"Yes, *we*," said Annot. "Holden is my cousin, and I fear him. But I know Dugald. He's weak, yes. He's never been allowed to be anything else. But he isn't stupid. And he is reasonable, and a good man, I think, at heart. You could talk to him, Your Grace, if you wanted to try again to make the peace your father and his wanted. Or you could, if Holden weren't there to tell Dugald what to think and what to do."

"I do not see that we shall have that chance," the queen said. Then she smiled, not in a happy way, but not unkindly, either. "Since you have so much to say on the subject, Baroness Oakhold, I ask that you join Prince Maurey in attending the council of war tomorrow morning after breakfast."

The queen rose, and an elderly knight came to take the sword from her. It must have been a ceremonial thing, like a sceptre, but I had no doubt that the queen could use it if she had to. It was clear in the way she held it, handing it to the man as familiarly and easily as Cook handled a carving knife in the Fowler College kitchen.

The queen turned back in the doorway.

"Maurey," she said, "my steward, Lady Ashell, will show you and the baroness to your rooms and see you have all you require. Her Eswyn is not very good, but Ashell does speak Ronish, and I believe as well-educated Dunmorrans you are both familiar with that language?"

"Yes, Your Grace." Annot answered for me as well. I hastily tried to call to mind all the Ronish I had once known.

"Good. So you should be able to understand one another."

The lady with the golden chain who had first led us in smiled

at me and bowed slightly. Poor Annot was still standing, listening
to voices in the dark. It was already hard to remember that. The
sun had set long ago, and no one had lit any candles.

"I would like it if you and Baroness Oakhold would join
us for breakfast in the morning, Maurey," the queen went on.
"You should meet the rest of your family."

Then she left, and the court broke up into murmuring clus-
ters of people. I went back to Annot and took her arm.

"It's a bit frightening," she muttered, "all these people wandering around in the dark. No, actually, I'm jealous. I wish I
had your eyes."

Aljess clapped her hands together, and a thin blue flame
appeared. Annot blinked and tried not to look surprised, and
I simply stared, gaping like a child seeing a juggler for the first
time.

"I'm so sorry, Annot," the knight said. "Baroness, I should
say. I didn't think of light for you. Lady Ashell will be sure you
have candles, you know. Ashell thinks of everything."

"Just call me Annot, please, Aljess. Do you Talverdine use
candles?"

"Of course. One cannot read in the dark! And using magic
for light is tiring. Although I once read about—"

"Tiring even if you are talented and like to show off, as Aljess
is and does," said Jessmyn, elbowing her sister. "Al, *they* are tired.
They no doubt want to bathe and eat and sleep, and Lady Ashell
would like to take them away and look after them."

"Indeed," the steward said in strongly accented Ronish. I
had to listen hard to let the words rise up from the memory
of distant lessons when I was a grammar-school pupil and not
a kitchenboy in Fowler College. "I'm sure the prince and the

baroness must be famished, as well as weary." She gave each of us another little bow.

"I'm sorry," Aljess said. "Of course. Good night, Maurey—Your Highness, I should say. Good night, Annot. I have to leave you in the dark, I'm afraid."

After a few more words with Lady Ashell in Talverdine, the twins strode off, their long mail shirts jingling. The thin blue flame went out like a blown candle as soon as Aljess turned away.

The steward touched Annot's arm. "May I guide you, Baroness? There will be a supper for you in your rooms, but after such a difficult journey as you have had, I am sure you must be wanting to bathe, first."

"They do keep mentioning baths," Annot whispered to me as she walked from the hall, one arm tucked through the steward's and the other through my own. "Do you think we smell?"

"I was hoping it was just Blaze," I said.

✳ CHAPTER TWELVE ✳
COUNCIL OF WAR

Breakfast with my new-found aunt and her family was both pleasant and awkward. Everyone was friendly, but we were all a little stiff, strangers with one another. I even felt like a stranger to myself. I was wearing clean new clothes for the first time in what seemed like forever: dark trousers, looser than the hose I was used to, and a linen shirt, with a tunic embroidered in scrolling dragons around the hem. I had new boots and in my belt a long knife with a heavy gilded hilt. My hair was combed and clean, held back from my face by a golden clasp. Annot too had new clothing in the Nightwalker style. Her tunic had running horses embroidered on it in red, and her skirt fell in folds from her hips, rather than flaring out over half a dozen petticoats in the Dunmorran fashion. It looked very elegant—*she* looked very elegant, all in green and brown with a touch of crimson, like some spirit of the forest, a votary of Vepris, though my tongue froze up when I thought of telling her so. She also had her knife in her belt; knives evidently did not count as the weapons she was not to carry in the royal presence, since the steward seemed to have provided a new sheath for it. Even Blaze was clean and fluffy, hardly recognizable as the same muddy, burr-matted dog he had been the night before. He lay with his head on Annot's boot, full of his own breakfast and snoring.

It was odd to think of myself as eating with my family, but a family meal it was. Queen Ancrena was married; her husband, Gelskorey, was a Maker, a magician as great as any in the land, though he said himself that his skill was nothing compared to what his grandmother's had been. He was a quiet gentle-seeming man, who reminded me of Harl Steward back at Dame Hermengilde's manor. Their daughter, the Crown Princess Imurra, was ten, a keen-eyed girl who seemed too old for her years as she listened to adult talk of war. I had a little boy cousin too, Prince Korian, but he was not yet out of diapers and was with his nurse that morning. *Family.* I smiled at Imurra, and after a moment she gave me a bright smile back.

Talk of war began with the clear broth made from bones or a little dried meat, the usual start to breakfast in Talverdin, and continued with bread and honey and fruit. We tried to talk of other things, of what it was like "living with humans" or of all the distant cousins, seconds, thirds and fourths, I seemed to have suddenly acquired, or of Annot's life at Oakhold, but somehow it always came back to Chancellor Holden and the threat from Dunmorra.

Servants—much more happy and clean than we at Fowler College had been, servants whom the queen and her husband spoke to by name and who answered with courtesy and without subservience—cleared away the breakfast dishes, and people other than family drifted in, finding seats around the long table. My new uncle Gelskorey, whose official title was translated as Consort, introduced each person as he or she arrived, but I could not keep all the strange names in my head. Some of the lords and ladies were councillors appointed by the queen, I gathered, while others were chosen by the people living in the kingdom's four districts.

Consort Gelskorey translated the Talverdine word for these districts as Quarterings. There were knights present as well, old and young, including Jessmyn and Aljess. Lady Ashell the steward arrived with her son Lord Hullmor, a cheerful-looking young man with a crooked nose and curly hair. Jessmyn hurried to take the chair across from him; Aljess rolled her eyes and grimaced as she pulled up a chair, gesturing for Annot and me to make room for her between us.

It was still almost unbearably strange and dreamlike to sit at that long table with nearly two dozen people around it and see all those black eyes looking at me, milk-white faces framed in coal-black hair.

To my relief, most of those black eyes were friendly this morning or at least curious. But one pair made me uncomfortable: a pair of eyes in a sharp thin face—a young man who scowled when he saw that I was watching him watching me and leaned to whisper something to the old man next to him. The old man had the same sharp features, but his expression was more closed, unreadable.

Not, I thought, a face any more friendly than the young man's, just a more careful one. Then I recognized the old man as the one who had called me a half-breed the night before.

"Who are they?" I whispered to Aljess, pointing in the direction of the scowling boy and the old man, with my hand flat on the tabletop so they would not see.

"Ah," she said, "Lord Roshing of Roshing Valley and his grandson, Romner. Lord Roshing is one of the two lords who represent the South Quartering on the Queen's Council." She chewed her lip, frowning thoughtfully. "He does not like humans much."

For a moment, Aljess looked as though she might say some-thing more about Lord Roshing. Then she nodded down the table to an older woman who had been introduced as Lady Ness of Dralla, governor of the port city. Apparently the Nightwalker kingdom still had a little contact with the outside world by sea, despite what we in the rest of Eswiland believed.

"That's my grandmother, Lady Ness."

There was something odd about the governor of Dralla, I thought, as she turned her head, speaking quietly with the Consort. I looked again, stared and realized I was being as rude as those people who used to stare at me. White skin, white-streaked black hair...

"She has blue eyes," I whispered to Aljess.

Her cheek dimpled. "So did my great-grandfather, her father," she whispered back. She glanced the other way at Annot and leaned even closer to me. "Your baroness isn't the first human sweetheart to run away to Talverdin, you know. My great-grand-father had red hair too."

"What about red hair?" Annot asked, while I sputtered and protested, "She's not—" But then Lady Ashell rapped on the table with a wooden rod or baton carved with oak leaves, and all fell silent. Queen Ancrena rose and began to speak.

She spoke in Talverdine, of course, but she had said very little before the sour-faced old man, Lord Roshing, rose to his feet. Lady Ashell looked at the queen, who frowned briefly and nodded. Lady Ashell pointed at Lord Roshing with her carved baton. It must have been some sort of official symbol giving him permission to address the council. He bowed to the queen.

"I must protest, Your Grace," he said. He spoke in Eswyn, very slowly and carefully as though to demonstrate how difficult or unpleasant it was to do so. And to make sure that Annot and I would understand his words. "This council is no place for humans. We meet to talk of war and invite the enemy to sit with us?"

"There are no enemies here, Roshing," the queen said.

"I see a murdering human and a half-breed human."

The queen's lips thinned, and her eyes narrowed. Blood rushed to the cheeks of Lady Ness of Dralla, and she swept to her feet, her stiff robes rustling.

"Perhaps I should leave then," she said, "if you don't wish to sit with those of human blood."

That took Lord Roshing by surprise—he must have forgotten about Lady Ness's human father, and the governor of Dralla was obviously an important woman, not someone to offend. Roshing's mouth opened and closed a couple of times, reminding me of nothing so much as the last narrow-faced pike I had caught in the Westwood.

Jessmyn and Aljess bounced to their feet as well.

"Us too," they said together.

"We wouldn't want to offend you with our human blood, my lord," Jessmyn almost purred. She looked like a wildcat about to sink claws into some little squeaking thing.

Young Lord Hullmor leaped to his feet, leaned over the table and said something to Lord Roshing in Talverdine. He sounded angry. Consort Gelskorey held his hand over his mouth. I think he might have been smiling. The queen simply stood with her arms folded while Lady Ashell pounded on the table with her baton and shouted something that silenced everyone.

They all sat again, except for Lord Roshing and the queen. Lord Roshing spoke to Lady Ness and bowed, smiling.

The half-human governor of Dralla did not smile back or

return the bow. "It is not only to me you should apologize," she said.

But Lord Roshing did not offer any apology to me or to Annot, who sat stiff and stony-faced.

"My nephew," the queen said, "*my nephew*, Prince Maurey, has every right to be here. As does his companion, Baroness Oakhold, who has lost her home and her position and risked her very life to save his. If you have nothing but insults to offer, you will be silent."

Lord Roshing's lips went very pale. He bowed and sat without another word. The youth beside him, his grandson Romner, smiled in a sneering sort of way, as though the whole situation amused him.

I was on my feet, the blood thumping in my ears. So many years I had spent trying not to be noticed, to be overlooked and forgotten, and here, surrounded by all those lords and ladies, in front of a queen, I was on my feet.

Lady Ashell, after a startled moment, waved at me with the baton.

I bowed to the queen. That seemed to be the correct way to begin. "Lord Roshing has called my friend a murderer," I said. I could hear my voice shaking. I know my hands were. I was gripping the edge of the table just to hold myself up. "Lady Ness is right. Lord Roshing should apologize to the baroness."

"Maurey!" Annot hissed. "It's all right. I don't care. He didn't mean me personally."

"That makes it worse," I said.

Jessmyn made a gesture like silent hands clapping.

"Lord Roshing?" the queen prompted in a voice of ice. The tone was enough to terrify me, but Consort Gelskorey gave me ever so slight a nod, and I realized he, and probably the queen as well, did not disapprove of my speaking up for Annot.

The old lord rose elegantly to his feet. The queen's voice did not seem to inspire any terror in him. He looked down his nose at Annot. "I apologize," Roshing said, "if I appeared to suggest that our new prince's little human…friend…was in any way involved in the many terrible massacres of our people by hers over the past five centuries."

And he sat down again. His grandson smirked. I sat down as well. I didn't know what to do. I felt like I had made things worse. He had managed to remind everyone of all the slaughter, the executions in the philosopher's fire, the horrible things humans had done to Nightwalkers since invading Eswiland. He had suggested Annot was…the way he said "little human friend" made her sound like some…some trollop, and, somehow, his whole apology was an insult.

Aljess squeezed my shoulder in encouragement, but I hunched down in my chair.

Annot rose to her feet, and Aljess reached for her arm, I think to drag her down before she could unleash any volley of insults against Lord Roshing. But Annot smiled, looking as dainty and charming as she ever had sitting reading in the garden. She dipped a deep curtsy.

"I accept Lord Roshing's apology," she said, looking at him through downswept lashes, "as sincerely as it was given. We can't choose our ancestors. If we could, no doubt some of us would be careful to pick ones with smaller ears."

She sat down again, and around the table people either looked confused, wondering if they were misunderstanding some odd Dunmorran proverb, or covered their mouths to hide smiles, as they looked at Roshing and Romner, who both had rather large ears. Romner's, which stuck out as much as any ears I had ever seen, slowly flushed red. He was no longer smirking.

Queen Ancrena cleared her throat. "I think," she said sternly, "it is time to turn our attention to more serious matters."

Almost all the rest of the council of war, which lasted until well after noon, was carried out in Talverdine. The queen spoke; other people rose and spoke; occasionally people raised their voices or thumped the table. No more angry insults were exchanged, though. Aljess whispered a translation to Annot and me, not of every argument, but enough so that we knew what was going on.

They discussed tearing down the halfworld bridge to hinder the advance of Holden's army and decided to do this only when his army entered the Westwood. The village militias would begin drilling at once, though, and as soon as the winter snows melted, knights would go out as scouts into the Westwood to report on the Dunmorran army's advance.

They also discussed sending an expedition deep into Dunmorra, as far as the city of Cragroyal itself, to try to retrieve the ring and prevent Holden from being able to get through the Greyrock Pass at all.

It was this proposal that caused most of the shouting and table-thumping. Many of the knights, even the elderly ones, were for it, but a number of the councillors thought it was too dangerous. Lord Roshing argued that Chancellor Holden and the king might not realize what the ring was, but that if a band of Nightwalkers tried to steal it back and were captured, the humans would be sure to know how much it mattered.

"But Holden already knows," Annot muttered when Aljess

translated this. "That's why Maurey and I had to tell the queen about it. I heard Holden talking about how the ring would let him wipe out the warlocks for good. That's why he's clearing the new road."

"Shh!" said Aljess, listening to the heated debate. "They know. That's what the Consort is saying now. And Roshing says it will simply mean that more good Talverdine die for nothing. He says that if the queen sends knights as spies into Cragroyal to find this ring, she is throwing their bodies into the philosopher's fire herself."

"How can he dare say that to her?" Annot whispered.

Aljess bit her lip and dropped her voice even lower, her face sober. "One of our ships was storm-wrecked on the coast of Eswy sixteen years ago, did you know? It was sailing to Rona. It was meant to be an embassy, to discuss perhaps opening up more trade. Most of the ship's company died. The six survivors were taken prisoner by Sawfield, a baron of the Eswyn king. He sent for men who knew how to make the philosopher's fire, to burn them, but they killed themselves before they could be burned. All six of them."

"How terrible," Annot breathed.

"Our parents were the ambassadors going to Rona," Aljess said. "My father drowned when the ship was wrecked, but my mother survived the wreck. Lord Roshing's son was captain of their knights. He was one of the survivors as well."

"Oh."

"So you see, that is why Lord Roshing feels so strongly against risking anyone's life beyond the mountains. He is always arguing against sending out spies and scouts and even fishing vessels that go beyond Dralla Bay. We are safe only here, he thinks."

"One can understand why he hates humans too," Annot said softly.

"Ah, no. Because then I would have to hate humans as well," Aljess said. "And I like the stories my grandmother tells of her father. My parents would never—they would never have wanted us to blame all humans for the actions of only some. But," she added, "some day, I think Jessmyn and I will go to Eswy and find that Baron Sawfield."

"Baroness Oakhold," the queen said in Eswyn, and all three of us jumped like naughty boys caught whispering in school. "You are kin to Chancellor Holden? Are you familiar with his home?"

"Yes, Your Grace." Nervously, Annot rose and bowed. She must have noticed that Nightwalker women did not curtsy, even when they were wearing skirts. "I lived with him for some time."

"Are you familiar with the palace and the university as well?"

"Much of it," Annot said cautiously.

"And Maurey, you know the secret ways under the university. You know of a hidden entrance to the city, the means by which you and the baroness escaped."

"Yes, Your Grace," I said.

"Could the two of you make a map to guide a small party of knights into the university and suggest the most likely places for the chancellor to keep such a treasure?"

She did not suggest that it was my duty to do so because it had been my father who began the whole tragic chain of events that let Holden get the ring. It was only I myself who felt responsible.

"I'll go with them," I said. "I'll do the searching. One person who knows the place well and can sneak around quietly will be better than a dozen clattering knights trying to read a map."

"We don't clatter," protested Jessmyn.

"I'll go too," Annot said. "I know Holden's house and the palace. Maurey doesn't."

"You'll betray our good knights to your king!" Roshing shouted.

"Dugald isn't the enemy!" I snapped to my own surprise. "And Annot faces as much danger as any warlock, going back to Cragroyal. They'll—" I stopped, not wanting to say it.

"I know," Annot said. "They'll behead me for a traitor and leave my head to rot on a spike over the city gate. I knew that when I rescued you."

"You can't go back!"

"It's no safer for you."

"It is not safe for anyone," Ancrena said quietly, and we both fell silent, sitting down again. "It is not safe for any of us. But if we do not retrieve that ring, Talverdin may be lost and there will be no safety for any Nightwalker, anywhere. Holden's hatred was plain, even when King Burrage was talking of friendship. It has only had time to grow since then. None of us will be safe, not the youngest infant, if he manages to come through the Greyrock Pass and fight his way into Talverdin. Baroness, I regret that I must do this and put someone so young to such risk. But I will accept your offer. And yours, nephew. You will be of the party that enters Cragroyal."

Aljess and Jessmyn bounded to their feet as one. Their grandmother sighed and covered her eyes, but I thought she looked rather proud.

"Yes, yes," the queen said, "I know."

"We speak several human languages," said Aljess.

"And Aljess is a Maker," added Jessmyn. "There should be a true warlock in the group. We'll need magic."

"And we've gone scouting in the Westwood many times."

"I said *yes*," the queen said. "Sit down."

They both sat, looking surprised.

Consort Gelskorey spoke then, and Lord Hullmor, the curly-haired son of the steward, rose and bowed.

"He's been put in charge of us," whispered Aljess. "Poor Hullmor."

Then Lord Roshing was on his feet again, speaking angrily. He was still arguing against the expedition as a waste of lives, saying that Annot was bound to betray the Nightwalkers, that she at least must remain in Talverdin. But his flow of words dried up entirely when his grandson, sneering eyes, smirking mouth, pointy nose, sticking-out ears and all, pulled his lanky body to his feet and said in perfect drawling Eswyn, "I'm going to Cragroyal too. You'll need a real warlock, if you're going to have any hope of getting back alive with that Eyiss-damned ring."

PART THREE

✳ CHAPTER THIRTEEN ✳
RETURN TO CRAGROYAL

Autumn was upon us before we reached Cragroyal. Although I had expected we would leave at once, it turned out there were many preparations to be made. Maps had to be consulted, spells studied, by Romner and Aljess at least, supplies and gear prepared, oafs—or so Annot called me, cheerfully, when she was not defending me against Jessmyn's friendly mockery—to teach to ride. Annot and I both endured lessons in the Talverdine language from the tutor of my young cousin Princess Immura, with Immura's less-than-helpful comments and to her unending amusement. When her tutor was out of earshot, the brat—I love my cousin dearly, but even she admits she was horrible at that age—delighted in teaching us words that were, to say the least, improper for court usage, though they came in very handy when I fell off my horse, as she and Annot were both quick to point out.

The heat of Morronas-month had passed before we left Sennamor Castle. It was early Aramin and the country folk were threshing the grain as we rode to the Greyrock Pass again. We crossed the pass in three days and crept by Greyrock Castle and the human town under cover of night. Our journey through the Westwood was swift and easy, as pleasant as a knight's journey in a ballad, with no foul weather, no wet fireless nights, no wandering in circles. As I had guessed and as their maps proved, the Nightwalkers knew the forest well. Autumn was beginning, crisp and dry, and we rode along narrow trails with the drifts of bright leaves rustling and crackling under our horses' hooves. We might have been out for pleasure, to picnic and gather nuts like fine ladies or to hunt the autumn-fat stags and boar. Blaze ran ahead, ploughing headfirst into leaf-drifts, chasing rustlings that might have been mice or squirrels or only the wind. Where Annot and I had wandered for over a month, we rode straight and true on little-used trails. We did not make such good time as the king's messengers might, since our trails grew more twisted the farther east we went; the more human farmsteads and villages there were, the more caution we used.

Annot and I were both learning to use a sword, though everyone agreed that the two of us would not go armed other than with our knives when we reached Cragroyal. Carrying weapons we could barely use would put us in even greater danger by making us seem to an enemy a greater threat than we were. Every evening we were given instruction, not always patiently, by Jessmyn, who hooted with laughter whenever we tripped ourselves or bashed our knuckles but always gave us a hand up and dusted us off. Back in Sennamor, Aljess had taught me much more about the halfworld, until I could fade in and out of it at will—so long as there was some shadow—as easily as drawing a breath. In the forest I was able to pull Annot and Blaze with me with no effort at all. Fortunately—or perhaps not—she did not need to hold my hand when we travelled in the halfworld, because the moon-white horses could cross between the layers of the world on their own, and carry a rider with them. As far as they were concerned, the halfworld was just another place, like walking around to the other side of a tree.

At night by the fire, Hullmor told us stories from the history of Eswiland before the days of Hallow's Conquest, his deep quiet voice holding us enthralled as we learned of great warriors and warlocks, adventurers and lovers from long ago. Jessmyn watched him, her eyes gleaming, and sometimes I would notice how Hullmor watched her out of the corner of his eye while he told the stories. And how Romner would scowl. But he scowled at everything.

Romner was the sour note in our journey, like a thorn you cannot get out of your sock, pricking and scratching with every step.

He laughed every time I fell off the patient white gelding with blue-gray ears that I had named Owlfoot. He jeered at Annot's sword practice and my own, told her that human girls were good for nothing but dressing like dolls and me that I was a soft, city-bred fop. When nothing important was at stake we tried to speak only Talverdine, to improve our mastery of the tongue, but he mocked our stumbling accents, mimicking us, particularly me. Whenever Aljess tried to work some small spell—to start a fire in the rain or use two crossed hazel-sticks to confirm where the next village lay so we could avoid it—Romner would watch with a little smile curling his upper lip. Then he would elbow her aside and do whatever it was she had been attempting, with an ease that made her look incompetent and ignorant. Aljess and Jessmyn called him a lout to his face, and Hullmor told him to keep silent if he could not be civil, but whenever they were out of earshot, Romner would start picking away at Annot and me again, his words like sharp stinging pebbles we could not dodge.

It would have been easier to take if he had not been so good at everything. He was as good as Jessmyn with a sword, though not as good as Hullmor, who was several years older than either of them. He could ride better than Annot. He spoke perfect Eswyn and Ronish, and he was, as he claimed, a far more powerful Maker, a better warlock, than Aljess.

I hated him. And yet, Romner treated the horses kindly and tenderly, showing more concern for their comfort than his own when we made camp. Several times I surprised him feeding Blaze treats saved from his own supper, rubbing the dog's ears and crooning to him. I hoped that when we reached Cragroyal, Romner would be left behind in the Westwood to guard the horses since he liked them so much.

No such luck was mine. The horses were sent into the halfworld, a spell whispered by Romner over each to make certain they stayed there rather than wandering out again to be seen by some passing Dunmorran. Blaze was sent after the horses, following a hot argument with Annot, settled by Hullmor, who was for once on Romner's side.

"He's right," the young lord said. "We don't need the dog to start barking at the wrong moment."

I had not realized it was possible for Blaze to stay in the twilight halfworld without some contact with a Nightwalker, but though it required a long and complicated-sounding spell, Romner staring deep into the dog's eyes, Blaze faded away into the night's blackness.

"They'll be safe," Romner said, not looking at any of us. "That foolish dog of the human's is a herd dog. He'll be perfectly happy staying with the horses, thinking he's in charge of them. If we don't come back in a few days, they'll know to make their own way home." Then he did look at me. "But I expect at least some of us will be coming back," he said. I thought it plain he hoped that some of us would not.

"That's enough," said Hullmor. "If we can't work together

and trust one another, the chances are none of us will come back. And if we fail, all Nightwalkers are doomed. We all know there simply aren't enough fighting men and women in Talverdin to stop a Dunmorran army, once it gets through the spells of the Greyrock Pass." He took a deep breath. "Are we ready? Annot, Maurey, you know this land, you lead the way."

The city gates were shut at night, and even in the halfworld we could not walk through stone walls. We slipped into the halfworld nonetheless and followed the route Annot and I had taken in our escape, from the edges of the Westwood, along the highway and down the steep shore to Cragfoot Lake.

Annot walked beside me, holding my hand so that we were joined like the dancers of Coldwater. They were a famous legend: six young men and women damned to dance hand in hand until the sea drowned the land and the stars burned out, cursed for merrymaking during the three solemn Shadow Days of Brotin-month when the worlds of the dead and the living drew nearest.

"Are the little sweethearts happy to be heading home?" Romner whispered behind us.

Quick as thinking, Annot stooped down, snatched up a stone from the lakeshore and flung it. Romner was too startled to duck. The stone struck him square in the chest. It clattered off harm-lessly—he was wearing a shirt of mail under his dark surcoat, like the others—but he yelped in surprise and snarled, "Bloody human rat!" half drawing his sword.

Hullmor thumped him between the shoulders. "Quiet!" he snapped. "Humans might not be able to hear us in the half-world, but you never know what their own magic might make possible."

"Bloody, stuck-up, South Quartering rat," muttered Aljess.

Through all this, Annot's grip on my hand never lessened.

"Come on," I whispered. "Ignore him. He's not worth getting upset about."

"I'm worth two of you, you—," Romner snarled.

This time Hullmor hit him not at all gently.

"Sorry," Annot whispered.

"For what?"

"You having to hold onto me. I feel so useless, like a piece of baggage."

"I don't mind," I said. "I mean..." I couldn't say I was glad of every chance I got to hold her hand.

Behind us, Romner sniggered. We could not whisper quietly enough to keep him from hearing. Those large ears had their uses.

Annot squeezed my hand.

We crawled into the cave mouth where the underground river emerged under the swinging curtain of ivy. The water level was lower than it had been early in the summer when Annot and I escaped; it had been a dry autumn. We waded along the secret river, not in the halfworld but just in the dark, with Aljess's blue tongue of flame hovering over Annot to light her path. Working our way under the lowest part of the roof was easier, and easiest for Annot and me, who were only wearing leather jerkins over our tunics and trousers. The others, wearing heavy, knee-length mail hauberks, had to be even more careful they did not get caught in the current and pulled under.

Then came the dangerous part. The most likely place to find the ring was around Chancellor Holden's neck.

It was a few hours after midnight. In the halfworld again,

Aljess's blue light extinguished, Annot and I led the way up into the Fowler College cellars, and from there into the college itself and out the scullery door. Romner and Aljess unlocked doors as we went, Aljess with a frown of concentration and much whispered muttering, Romner with a flick of his finger and a superior sneer.

"I could kick his ankle, if you like," Annot whispered to Aljess and won a tired smile from her.

The door of the chancellor's house opened as easily as any other. We had agreed that only Hullmor, Annot and I would go inside, while the other three guarded our retreat. Following Annot's pointing finger, we slipped up the stairs to the second floor and Holden's bedchamber.

He was asleep, snoring faintly behind the heavy curtains of the wide bed, which were only barely visible in the halfworld. Holden seemed to be behind a barrier no thicker than a cobweb. The room itself was paneled in many different-colored woods, and in the halfworld each kind had a different gray sheen to it, a different shimmering tone, more like music than color. It was indescribably beautiful, and for a moment all I could do was stare, entranced.

Sword in hand, Lord Hullmor reached through the insubstantial curtains and brushed, ever so lightly, his left hand over Holden's neck. Then he stood back, shaking his head.

The ring on its chain was not there.

I began searching the room. Annot tugged me over to the mantelpiece and took the key to Holden's jewel-chest from a small alabaster pot. I looked through all his jewels, while Hullmor stood by the bed, sword ready, in case the chancellor woke up. I found a heavy chain of office with the Great Seal of Cragroyal University hanging from it, and a dozen other rings whose stones gleamed with silver and pearly light, colorless in the halfworld, but no heavy ring with a square stone carved with an oak leaf, no thick chain familiar from all the years I had worn it around my neck. We searched the shelves of the clothespress and found nothing but clothing and a bag of cedar bark to keep away moths. Neither did we find what we sought in the deep chest that held winter furs and woollens, or on the mantelpiece over the fire. I even knelt by the bed, my heart hammering so loudly I thought Holden would surely hear, and slid my hand under the pillows.

There was nothing for it but to search the rest of the house.

Master Arvol had rooms in the college, but he preferred to live in the chancellor's luxurious house. We left his room, by the head of the stairs, for later. Neither Annot nor I thought Holden would trust his brother with something that represented as much power as the ring did. Instead, we started our new search downstairs in the chancellor's study. Annot slipped her hand from mine, fading to ghostly reality in the night-dark real world.

"What are you doing?" I demanded, reaching for her, but she expected that and ducked away, even though I was invisible to her.

"I want to look at his workroom," she said, answering the question she knew I had asked, though she had not heard it. She held up another key that she must have taken from the alabaster pot in the bedroom. "I was never allowed in there, and I never dared steal the key before. I'll be back in a moment."

Hullmor and I began searching the bookshelves and the clutter of papers and parchments on the writing desk. We had to step back into the real night-dark world, because our half-world fingers could not grip the misty books to pull them out.

Somehow even my heartbeat seemed twice as loud, knowing that
I was visible.

I found the Fowler College account book, left open as though
someone had been working on it, and carried it over to the window
where pale moonlight drifted in. It looked to me as though Master
Arvol was spending rather a lot of money meant for the running
of the college on a wine cellar and his own table. Turning the
pages back through the years, I found an entry with my name:
"Maurey Hermengildesward." Proof that my fees had been paid,
enough to see me through grammar-school and my degree and
witnessed by the college master and the former bursar, who had
died six months later. And after that, yes, after that, spending
began to increase. Sums were noted as withdrawn here, there…
It was a small thing, but it mattered to me to prove Master Arvol
had stolen from Dame Hermengilde. I tore out that page and
shoved it down the front of my tunic.

"What are you doing?" Hullmor whispered. "Where's that girl
gone? We can't go wandering all over. Go get her back."

I followed the slate-floored corridor Annot had taken and
jumped, hand on my knife, when the darkness thickened and
turned into Romner, sword in hand and eyes gleaming.

He sniggered. "Scared, human boy?"

"You're supposed to be guarding the front door."

"Boring out there. I thought a real warlock might be more
use in here. Where's the other one?"

"If you mean the baroness, I'm just going to find her."

Romner shrugged and fell in beside me. "No ring?" he
asked.

"Not yet."

"I'm not surprised. Think about it. Holden finds the ring that will let him into Talverdin so he can kill all the warlocks his heart desires, big bad warlock escapes in a cloud of pig dung with his precious ward and is never recaptured…of course he has to suspect that you might have gone to Talverdin. Of course he's expecting, if that's the case, that we'll come back for the ring. He won't leave it hanging around his neck where dear Hullmor can just stab him in the heart and take it."

"Where is it, then?" I asked. "Since you know so much about it."

Romner failed to say anything biting. He just frowned. "If it were me," he said, "I'd use it as bait in a warlock trap."

"He might," I said. "You and Holden have the same nasty sort of mind."

For a moment I almost thought Romner looked hurt.

"Anyone intelligent could have figured that out," he said, sneering again. "Anyone intelligent might ask a Maker who actually has a bit of power to cast a spell to find the stupid ring."

"Well, if you can do that, do it and stop boasting," I snapped. I pushed open the heavy door at the end of the corridor. "Annot?"

"In here," she whispered.

Romner, silent now, followed me into a cold, damp-smelling room with a flagstone floor. To my night vision, the floor was the same creamy, streaky, shell-scattered stone of some of the deep tunnels under the university. Annot had lit a candle, but beyond her little pool of golden light the room glittered with the night colors of glass, some of it faintly blue but much a venomous green. Glowing metal frames held many of the vessels sitting on the burn-scarred benches. There were odd-shaped flasks of murky liquids, alembics for distilling, porcelain and stone mortars and pestles for grinding, crucibles...

"A laboratory for alchemy," Romner said, sounding impressed. "Well-stocked too." He began to prowl along the benches.

"What did you bring him for?" Annot asked.

"He followed me. Any sign of the ring?"

"Not so far. Maurey—I wasn't really looking."

"What were you looking for, then?"

"This." Her voice shook, and she held out the candlestick, pointing without touching.

Shelves lined one wall, with dark-glazed pottery jars ranged neatly on them. All the jars were tightly stoppered, some with cork, some sealed as well with lead. They were labeled mostly in Ancient Ronish, the formal language of the philosophers and astrologers that was ancestor to the tongue spoken in the empire now, but some of the paper labels carried only alchemical symbols I had not yet studied enough to understand.

"This jar." Annot did touch one; a jar smaller than most and white in color. Its paper label, in the candlelight, said simply, "Tonic."

"What about it?"

"Cousin Holden had that when he came to Oakhold. I saw it there, and I asked about it. He said it was a stomach tonic that he took sometimes and that little girls shouldn't be so nosy." Her voice shook. "But I know I saw him mixing it in my mother's wine once. I thought it was medicine, then. I mean, I believed him about it being a stomach tonic. But now—I think that's how he poisoned her."

"Who poisoned whom?" asked Romner, leaning over her shoulder to pick up the jar. It was only corked, not sealed. He opened it and sniffed. His eyes were bright with interest.

"Go away," I said. "Her mother's death isn't a joke."

Romner stuck a finger in the jar and carried some of the fine white powder away on his fingertip into the darkness. I followed, half-expecting that he would taste it and laugh at Annot's fears.

The powder had its own rich, oily, brownish-black glow in the darkness.

"I certainly wouldn't take this for my stomach," Romner said, without any trace of a sneer. "It's stibium, I think."

"What's that?" we both asked.

"Poison," he said. "How did your mother die?"

Hesitantly, still expecting some sharp comment, Annot told him. Romner listened, frowning, and rubbed the white powder off onto a dirty rag from one of the tables.

"Pity there's no way to prove it now," he said. "If you'd known, there's a test alchemists use in Rona when it's suspected someone has been poisoned. You know how common poison is as a weapon in clan feuds down there, or so they say. Stibium and arsenic, poisons of that sort, they can be given in smaller doses so that it looks like the person died of a natural illness—but when the poison is given that way, it builds up in their hair and their fingernails. An alchemist can detect the poison if it's there."

"But," Annot said slowly, "I do have some of my mother's hair."

"Ah," said Romner.

"There's nothing we can do about that now," I said sharply. And I could have kicked myself. Here was Romner actually acting friendly for a change, and I went and snapped at him because—I had to admit it—I didn't like the way Annot was looking at him as though he had just offered her a great gift.

"Have you studied alchemy, Romner?" Annot asked.

"Some," he said, with a trace of his sneer returning. "More than His Highness, even though I haven't been to university."

"Neither have I," I said. "Where did you get that idea? I thought you were listening when I told the queen my story. I was a scullion here, not a scholar. I don't know any alchemy at all, and if you do, and can help Annot find out what happened to her mother, then do it for her sake and not to prove you're better than me. We all know you are, anyway."

He gave me a cold look down the length of his nose and opened his mouth. I never found out what he was going to say, because at that moment there was a horrible bang, like the worst sort of student alchemical experiment gone wrong. It was followed by a great noise and clatter, people shouting, booted feet running, glass breaking. A handbell clanged urgently, starting upstairs and hurrying down, rattling the windows.

One of the shouting voices was Lord Hullmor's.

I blew out Annot's candle, plunging the room into darkness, grabbed her by the arm and, taking a deep calming breath, drew her into the gray light of the halfworld. Romner was already gone, running down the corridor, cloaked in shadows, his sword in his hand.

We raced after him.

❄ Chapter Fourteen ❄
The Chancellor's Trap

"It's a trap! Get out of here!"

The Talverdine words were clear, even over the echoes of the bell. Annot and I hesitated in the corridor. Romner stood in the study doorway, flattened against the doorframe as if he did not trust the halfworld to hide him, but it was Hullmor's voice we had heard.

The front door burst open and Jessmyn, gray and ghostly, not in the halfworld, edged in, sword drawn. She looked around and hurled herself though the doorway to the study.

An arm, Romner's, grabbed her into the halfworld with us.

"Stay back!" he hissed.

For a moment I thought Jessmyn might turn her sword on him. Then she gave a jerky nod and shrugged his hand off. Annot and I pressed up behind them, trying to see.

Annot gave a little moan and pressed her free hand over her mouth. Hullmor and Aljess were in the far corner of the room by the fireplace. Dead white light flickered over them from a curving line of flames that rose from the floor, neat as if drawn by a compass. Philosopher's fire, I realized, even as I felt a strange queasy chill in my blood. To us they were both a bit faint and foggy to look at, no longer in the halfworld, trapped by the cold white fire.

Chancellor Holden, in his nightgown, with a sword in one hand and a candle in the other, and Master Arvol, a blanket over his shoulders, carrying in one hand a candelabrum with all its five candles lit and in the other a big handbell, stood in the center of the room. Beside them were four royal men-at-arms in breastplates and helmets, carrying swords and halberds. The men stood in a scatter of glinting broken glass, showing how they had gotten in. Summoned by the bell, I assumed. A cold wind curled in the shattered window, blowing the curtains.

"That ring is an imitation, warlocks," Chancellor Holden said, "a piece of magic of my own, with which I'm quite pleased. You probably cannot appreciate the amount of research it was necessary to do, to discover how to keep a philosopher's fire hidden and dormant, to be triggered only when someone took the ring from the tinderbox there. A nice, obvious hiding place, I thought. I was sure you wouldn't miss it. Although I did expect it would be Rhodora's little monster who came back for it."

"Get away," Hullmor said, speaking Talverdine still, which I could follow reasonably well by then, although I spoke it with an appalling accent. He made his voice conversational, as if he was explaining to Holden that he couldn't understand. "The ring isn't here. They were expecting us to try to get it back. Those guards were waiting someplace nearby, and more are probably coming."

Jessmyn shook her head, although he couldn't see her.

"Do what he says," Aljess muttered, and we could barely hear her. Her voice was weak, and she swayed on her feet. Hullmor caught her by the elbow, but then he dipped his head. It was hard to tell which of them was supporting the other. Then they both crashed forward, one falling and pulling the other down.

We all jumped towards them. I think we had the same thought, that they were going to break out through the pale flames, but I at least should have known better. To the others the philosopher's fire was just a terrible story, but I had experienced its effects and knew it did not even have to touch Nightwalkers to do them—us—harm. Both were nearly fainting, too sick to stand.

"Get them out!" Jessmyn screamed, and she slipped into the visible world for a moment, before Romner grabbed her back again.

"There's more!" Master Arvol shouted. "Help! Warlocks!" He began clanging his handbell again and held the candelabrum high, waving it so the shadows danced and ran.

Chancellor Holden shouted orders at the soldiers. Two of them dragged Hullmor and Aljess right through the line of white flames. Aljess twitched and screamed and went limp again, and Hullmor jerked like a hooked fish. They were quickly bound, hand and foot, and bundled out the window to more men-at-arms who were running up with torches. They must have been stationed nearby in a Fowler College dormitory, to be ready if the chancellor's trap was sprung.

The other two soldiers and the chancellor rushed for us.

"No!" I shouted as Jessmyn sprang to meet them, teeth bared. "Romner, stop her!"

I could do nothing myself. If I let go of Annot, she would be seen.

"Light!" Master Arvol was yelling. "We need more light!" He dropped the bell, grabbed a jar off the mantelpiece and hurled it into the fire. The fire roared up, hot and blinding, flooding the room with white light and driving the shadows away.

It was not philosopher's fire but merely the whiteness of any flame when seen from the halfworld, but I ran with the shadows, dragging Annot, and Romner hauled Jessmyn after us.

"Let me go!" she shouted. "They'll kill them!"

"Shut up!" Romner yelled. "What if they hear you?"

"Both of you shut up!" Annot screamed as we stumbled out the front door.

"Quiet!" I ordered in a whisper. And they all fell silent. Tears ran down Jessmyn's face, and Romner's cheek had a deep red mark where she had hit him with her fist and the hilt of her sword. At least she had not used the blade. Annot reached out with her free hand and clasped Jessmyn's. Romner let go of the knight and rubbed his face, scowling.

"We follow them," I said. "But we have to keep our heads. When we're in the halfworld, they can't drive us out—that's right, isn't it? Even bright firelight, even daylight?" That was what Aljess had told me: we only needed night or deep shadow as a gateway of sorts, to and from the halfworld. Once we were in we stayed there, even in broad open daylight. Back in that room with the brilliant alchemical fire lighting it like noon, I had not wanted to take a chance.

"Of course," Romner said.

"You put a spell on Blaze, to send him into the halfworld on his own, without anyone touching him," I went on. "Why can't you do the same for Annot?"

He blinked and looked down at his feet. His ears turned a darker shade of gray as he flushed.

"No one asked me," he said.

"You utter—!" Jessmyn could not seem to think of any words terrible enough.

Annot just shook her head. "Do it," she said. "We all need our hands free for weapons now."

"If Romner had stayed out on guard like he was supposed to," Jessmyn started to say.

"It's not my fault Hullmor set off the trap. Any fool could have guessed the chancellor would plan something like that. And if Aljess had stayed outside, she wouldn't have been caught."

"She went looking for you!"

"That's enough!" I said. "Keep your voices down!" Though remembering how I had shouted to Annot after I crossed the halfworld bridge, I doubted the loudest scream could carry back to the daylight world, at least for human ears to hear.

More royal guardsmen were converging on the chancellor's house by the minute, and students and masters from nearby Fowler College were gathering too, awakened by the noise and stir. Servants, who would already have been up as I knew too well, mingled with them, enjoying the excuse to put off work. The four of us crept in under the shelter of the hedge for the feeling of safety it gave as the pale dawn light ate up the darkness.

"It's the same spell as the one I put on your dog," Romner warned. "You'll stay in the halfworld until one of us draws you out."

"Just do it," Annot repeated.

Romner squatted down in front of her as he had with Blaze, staring into her eyes and holding her with a hand on each side of her head. He was surprisingly gentle about it.

"Woof," Annot muttered, but even she didn't look like she thought it very funny.

This time I listened closely to the words Romner spoke. His spell was in Talverdine. It was quite simple, really. Although it was structured like a poem, the words merely told Annot, or the power that was in Romner, what was going to happen. The human Annot would stay in the halfworld, unseen by human eyes, would walk safely cloaked in darkness and shadow...I could almost see the shape of what was happening, the way the world twisted itself a little to follow the Maker's words.

"Let go of her hand, Maurey," Romner said. I think it was the first time he had ever used my name.

We all held our breath when I let go. Nothing happened. Annot was already in the halfworld. She stayed there with us. We all sighed with relief, and I rubbed my stiff cramped hand. Annot did the same.

"You'll have to think of other excuses to hold on to her now," Romner said. Did he sound...jealous?

Jessmyn wiped her eyes with her surcoat. "What now, Maurey?"

Even Romner looked at me expectantly.

"We need to find where they've taken Aljess and Hullmor," I said slowly. "And we still need to find the ring."

"The palace," Annot said. "The dungeons?"

I closed my eyes for a moment, trying to remember all the chaos and confusion in the study, Holden shouting...

"Holden told the men-at-arms to take them to the king," I said. "They may—they may not wait for long before they execute them if they're afraid there are more of us who might rescue them."

"Straight to the palace, then," Jessmyn said grimly. "We can look for the Eyiss-damned ring later."

"Hullmor would say the ring was more important," said Romner. When no one said anything, he went on angrily, "Well, it is. If Holden has that ring, all Talverdin may die, not just two people."

"She's my *sister*," Jessmyn said.

Neither Annot nor I said anything. I realized both Jessmyn and Romner were looking at me.

"She's my sister," Jessmyn said again, pleadingly. "I can't leave her to die."

I suddenly remembered Annot talking about a baron's duties to his people, and to his king. I wished I had not remembered, just then.

I was a prince. Queen Ancrena had called me that, acknowledged me as her nephew in front of the lords and ladies of her kingdom. She had trusted me enough to send me on this mission, trusted me to help save the people of Talverdin, who would not be in such deadly danger if my father—no—if both my parents had been strong enough to put their people ahead of their own desires.

"We need to find the ring and get it out of Chancellor Holden's reach," I said quietly, looking down at my hands clenched on my knees. "I'm sorry. That's what we were sent to do."

I swallowed and looked up at Jessmyn. There were tears in her eyes again. "Once we find the ring, two of us will take it back to Talverdin. Two can stay to look for Hullmor and Aljess, and rescue them if we can."

Jessmyn stared down at the ground. After a moment she nodded.

"Yes, sir," she said.

✳ Chapter Fifteen ✳
Return to the Hall of Judgement

We stood in a shadowy corner of the palace's main courtyard, wondering where to go next.

"Nothing," Romner said in disgust. He held an odd tangle of sticks in his hand—twigs he had cut from the yew hedge under which we had sheltered—lashed together with strands of my hair. He had needed to use my hair, he said, because I had carried the ring for so long and therefore had a greater connection to it than the rest of us. But though he had murmured over the twigs the whole time he wove and knotted them together, telling them they were going to be attracted to the ring that was the key to Greyrock Pass, that they would twist and tug and draw us to it, his creation, like a sort of triangular wooden spiderweb, lay inert across his palms.

"It should have worked," he said angrily. "It's not my fault. If it won't work for me, it wouldn't work for anyone less powerful than the Consort himself, and he's not here. There's just no power left in us anymore for complicated spells like this. We're weak. We're hardly fit to be called warlocks. The stupid humans might as well burn us all."

"Don't say that," said Jessmyn, her teeth clenched. "Let me try."

"You? You have no Maker's talent at all."

"Very well. We can't find the ring. I'm going to look for Aljess and Hullmor."

"Wait," I ordered and was surprised when Jessmyn did so, folding her arms and scowling.

"You searched for villages in the Westwood easily enough, Romner," I said. "Why doesn't this spell work? It looks like the same type of thing."

"Searching for villages means searching for groups of people," Romner said, his tone of voice suggesting I was a complete idiot for asking. "It's much simpler to detect living things. They disturb the currents of power in the world far more than something small and inert. If we were closer, I could probably feel the power of the spells in the ring, even without using a spell myself. But we aren't close enough."

"But your—whatever you call it—your sticks are glowing," I said. "The spell must be reacting to something."

Romner looked at me and down at the construction of yew twigs in his hands. "Glowing?" he asked. "No, they aren't. And they aren't supposed to, anyway."

But the twigs *were* glowing. A faint, warm, greenish light flowed along them, like a slow-moving trickle of water, which was doubly strange, since I had never before seen color in the halfworld.

"We're wasting time," Romner said, and he threw the twigs down. "We'll simply have to search the whole palace." He glanced at Jessmyn. "Perhaps we'll find the others too."

I bent down and picked up the spellbound twigs and almost dropped them again as a spark jumped across to my hand.

"What was that?" Annot asked.

I held the twigs the way I had seen Romner do, across the palms of my upturned hands, thumbs gently resting on the two main pieces of the frame. The green light began to wind around my hands, and I felt an odd heat, more in my left hand than my right.

"Your spell *is* working, Romner," I said.

"For you? It can't be." He frowned and laid a finger on the twigs again. "You're no Maker."

"How do you know he isn't?" asked Annot.

"He's a half—." Romner cut the word off and shrugged. "His mother was human."

"There are human warlocks," Annot pointed out. "Up in the fens in the north you find men and women who work magic with hardly any training at all beyond what they get at their mother's knee, not alchemists and philosophers trained in the secret arts in universities. They call themselves witches. I have distant kin who are Fenlanders. I've seen a mere child, my third cousin Korby—he was my foster-brother for a couple of years when we were younger—do things I could hardly believe. Though the philosophers say they're almost as wicked as Nightwalkers, of course."

"That's different." Romner scowled. "*Maurey* can't be. He's no Fenlander. Besides, if that spell won't work for me, there's no way it would work for him."

"Maybe it's because you used my hair in it," I suggested. We had no time for arguments. "It feels like…it's to the left, the oldest wing of the palace." I pointed with the twigs, and they almost seemed to tug at my hands.

"Let's go," said Jessmyn. She started forward, the rest of us following. Romner grumbled that I was imagining it, but I don't think he believed himself.

We did not even have to enter the palace to learn where the ring was. A pair of broad doors, closed now, with men-at-arms on guard duty before them, made the twigs in my hands grow almost too hot to hold, and I had to grip them tightly. They felt like they might fly out of my grasp.

"The Hall of Judgement," said Annot.

"We should have some pigs," I said, and she flashed me a nervous smile.

Annot led us around by back doors and narrow passages until we were in the corridor behind the hidden side door through which both we and the king had escaped before. Peering through the keyhole, I could see the king's throne and Dugald sitting on it. Slightly blurred and ghostly though he was, I could see he looked pale and unhappy. As I watched, he yawned and rubbed his eyes. His hair was tousled as though he had just gotten out of bed. Probably he had. He was wrapped in a scruffy, fur-lined green robe that even at its best had never been formal court costume. Somehow his un-kingly shabbiness served to emphasize how young and alone he really was. But my moment of brotherly sympathy was brief. Beyond Dugald was a metal stand, a brazier such as one might burn incense on, as an offering to the shades in an ancestor shrine. This one, though, burned with a snapping white flame, which hummed a high clear note. Philosopher's fire.

The yew twigs burned in my hand, and I did drop them, then, not surprised to see they were charring. Romner stamped on them.

There was something in the middle of the flames on the brazier: a small block of stone, and a glint of silver light on it that I knew was actually gold.

"The ring's there," I said. "It's surrounded by philosopher's fire."

I leaned sideways, trying to peer down the length of the hall. Yes. Hullmor and Aljess. They were on their feet now, but their hands were still bound, and their swords had of course been taken. Hullmor's face was dark with bruising, as though he had been beaten or trampled, and Aljess' hands were stained with blood that trickled down one sleeve.

Then I could see nothing at all except the back of a dark robe as Chancellor Holden moved up to talk to the king.

"It must be done without delay," he was saying.

"No," King Dugald said. "I want to talk to them."

"You mustn't, Your Grace." That was Master Arvol's voice, barely remembering he addressed his king and not some schoolboy, from the sound of it. "The warlocks' words will bespell you. Remember what happened last time."

"Yes," the king said, "I do remember. You, warlocks. Do you speak Eswyn?"

Neither of them answered.

"What happened to the…the other one? Last spring. Do you know?"

They said nothing.

"His name is Maurey. Please, I just want to know if he's safe. And the girl too."

"Your Grace!" said Holden. "You risk contaminating yourself further with the warlocks' evil. There are already enough rumors spreading around the kingdom about your relationship with that other one. People believe you let him escape. They whisper that you've fallen prey to a warlock spell. Think how your people will feel if they learn you still suffer this—unfortunate disability. A nation cannot be led by a man so tainted by evil."

"Dugald needs to be rescued as much as Hullmor and Aljess," Annot muttered, her ear, like Jessmyn's and Romner's, pressed to the crack of the door.

"The king? He's the one who's going to burn them," hissed Jessmyn.

"He's my brother," I said.

Holden moved away, and I peered down the great hall again, as best I could. I could see four guards surrounding Aljess and Lord Hullmor, and two more inside the great doors. Two beyond the brazier. All wore steel cuirasses and helmets and mail hose, expecting trouble, it seemed. Candelabra were ranged down both sides of the hall, driving away the shadows where morning light from the high windows did not fall. There were no other councillors, no courtiers, no clerks. No one at all to witness this judgement on the warlocks. Perhaps Holden did not want to risk anyone hearing Dugald say anything sympathetic to them, or anything about me.

I wondered how many people really believed Dugald under a spell. There was an odd twin nature to beliefs about warlocks out among the country folk. We just never thought about it, even while we sang the ballads. They were evil, they would emerge from the shadows and cut your throat—but it was very sweet and tragic and romantic, how Queen Rhodora had run away with the handsome warlock prince. People might think more about the romance and the tragedy and less about the evil, if their king seemed to treat Nightwalkers as people, the same as humans.

But Holden would not stand for that. He wanted to be a great conqueror, like Good King Hallow, a champion of humanity, exterminator of warlocks.

"Eight guards," I said. "Plus the two outside, I suppose, who'll come in if there's any noise. Chancellor Holden and Master Arvol—they're not fighters. And Dugald, the king. There are four of us and only two warriors."

"Pity you can't do some real magic, Romner," Jessmyn said cruelly. "You could just put them all to sleep."

We were outnumbered, but we had to try. It was likely that the brazier of philosopher's fire never went out, and it would be guarded day and night, until Holden took the ring again to lead his armies to the Greyrock Pass. And none of us, no matter how well we understood that the ring was more important than any two lives, could stand here and wait while Aljess and Hullmor were burned alive.

"One of us grabs the ring," I said, "and gets out of here. Then the rest of us will try to free Hullmor and Aljess."

"How do you suggest we grab the ring?" Romner asked, his voice sneering at its worst. "I suppose you suddenly know a spell against philosopher's fire?"

Annot gave a hiccough of laughter. "Why, Romner, are you counting me as a Nightwalker? That's rather sweet, in a strange sort of way."

"I—but—." And he laughed, quietly, without malice. "I forgot."

He did not suggest that she would give the ring to the king or Holden, or betray us in some other way.

"Ride hard and fast for the Greyrock Pass," he said, instead. "Don't wait for the rest of us."

"I know," she said.

But of course, few plans go as intended once the enemy becomes involved.

✳ CHAPTER SIXTEEN ✳
DUGALD

It was not much of a plan, but it was all we had.

The door was not locked. I lifted the latch and nudged it open. No one noticed. All eyes were on the king, who had risen to his feet.

"Tell me where Maurey is," Dugald was saying, "and I swear, by my father's shade, that I'll let you go free."

"Your Grace!" Holden said. "You don't know what you're saying. Perhaps you should return to your chambers."

"No," Dugald said, sounding not so much like a king as like a little boy refusing to go to bed.

"Your mind is disturbed, Your Grace. The warlocks must be burned to cleanse the land of the evil they bring."

"No one is going to be burned!" Dugald shouted. "I won't have it! No more burning!"

"His Grace the king is not himself," Master Arvol said, addressing the guards by the brazier. "I think it would be best if he withdrew."

The two men-at-arms looked at one another uncertainly as the four of us slipped out into the Hall of Judgement. Like a ghost, Annot darted around the edge of the room towards the brazier.

And recoiled, a look of horror and pain on her face. I ran to her. She was pale and shaking.

"Powers save me!" she said in a whisper, through teeth still clamped on a cry of pain. "That philosopher's fire burns! I thought humans couldn't feel it."

"They can't," I said. "I've never heard that they could."

Even at a distance of several yards, I could feel it reaching for me. The blood began to ring in my ears, and I drew Annot back.

She swallowed. "I'm in the halfworld, Maurey. That must be why the fire affects me."

"You'll be seen..."

"It's the only way."

We would both be seen. Romner had said one of us must draw her out of the halfworld to break his spell. I did not know how to push her out.

There was a little shadow behind the throne, running over the floor and up the wall. I slipped back to the daylight world, watched colors flood back to full bright life.

"Annot?" I whispered, no more than a breath, and held out my hand to where I knew she was. She took it and was there beside me. But the shadow was too thin, the sunlight strengthening with every passing moment. I could not return, not there.

"Go," I whispered.

Annot nodded and ran. I could see how she braced herself as she approached the brazier, anticipating, flinching, from the pain she had felt before. But the philosopher's fire did not bend towards her. It remained even and white. She was plunging her hand through it, snatching up the ring on its chain, before the guards had time to believe their eyes and react.

Being good Dunmorran soldiers, they had trouble imagining a pretty girl as an enemy, anyway.

"Hey!" one exclaimed. "You! What are you doing?"

"Annot?" Master Arvol yelped, while the men-at-arms were still staring, reaching, looking confused.

"Annot!" Chancellor Holden shouted. "You! Stop her, you fools! A traitor, stop her!"

Annot ran straight for the door in the paneling. There was no one in the dimness beyond to pull her to invisibility in the halfworld. Jessmyn and Romner had run to Aljess and Hullmor, as soon as they saw Annot had the ring. They tumbled from the halfworld themselves—I suppose it would have been dishonorable to attack the guards while safe and unreachable themselves in the halfworld, but it would have been more practical. Or perhaps, like the books, the flesh of the guards would have been too ghostly to be contacted by halfworld blades. Swords sliced through rope. Jessmyn spun away and kicked one of the guards down; Aljess seized his sword. Hullmor crashed into the soldier who was swinging his blade at Romner, and both the young lord and the Dunmorran fell. When Hullmor bounced to his feet again, that soldier's sword was in his hand and Romner was back to back with him fighting off another.

I leaned from behind the throne and tripped the first of the men pursuing Annot. The second swerved away, and as I jumped to pursue him, the first seized me by an ankle, sending me crashing to the floor. I rolled, kicking at him to get free, and found myself staring up into my brother's startled blue eyes.

Then he bent, plucked the knife from my belt, and ran after Annot.

"No!" I screamed and pulled free of the soldier, scrambling to my feet. I lurched after the king in time to see him overtake the man behind Annot, grab him by the shoulder, knock his helmet off and thump him, hard, behind the ear with the heavy hilt of my knife. The man clanged as he crumpled up senseless on the floor.

"Hah!" Dugald said with great satisfaction. He turned back to the knot of fighters in the center of the hall and roared, "Stop!" in a voice that rattled the windows far above.

Everyone froze. Even Annot turned in the doorway, on the threshold of escape to the cellar tunnels, and stood there.

"Put down your weapons!" Dugald commanded in the same thunderous voice. "All of you."

"No more burnings," he said in a quieter tone, which nevertheless carried to the far reaches of the Hall of Judgement, where the guards who had been outside stood by the open doors. One had already laid down his halberd. After a moment, the other did as well. But the fighters all still gripped their swords. Aljess' arm was still bleeding. I could see the stain seeping through where several links in the sleeve of her mail shirt were torn open. One of the king's men knelt on the floor, Jessmyn's sword at his throat. Another lay at Hullmor's feet, his face nearly as white as mine, but he was still breathing, I could see.

"No more burning," Dugald said again. "I said, lay down your weapons!"

"The king is bespelled!" Master Arvol shouted, but it came out as more of a squeak, and no one paid him any attention.

A sword clattered as a man-at-arms, after one look at the king's face, dropped it. The one who had grabbed me laid his sword down and lurched wincing to his feet. Then Aljess, carefully, her eyes never leaving the soldier she faced, laid down her sword. That man did the same, backing away from her.

"Jess!" she prompted, and Jessmyn too laid down her blade, taking her sister's hand. Hullmor set his very carefully at his feet, and finally, Romner, with a snort and a scowl at me as though it was somehow my fault, wiped his sword on his surcoat and sheathed it, which was not quite what the king had ordered. Romner folded his arms as if to say he took no further interest in what was happening.

Chancellor Holden's eyes glittered. "Seize the warlocks!" he ordered. "Seize the king, for his own safety."

A couple of the men-at-arms looked at one another and at the king, who was swinging my knife in his hand. They stayed where they were.

"I have no quarrel with the warlocks," Dugald said, almost as if to himself. "*Dunmorra* has no quarrel with the warlocks. My mother was a willing partner in her elopement, not a victim of abduction. Old wars should be left for the historians, not reborn with every generation." He scowled at us all and tucked my knife into the sash that belted his robe. "I will have peace with Talverdin," he said. "Baroness Oakhold, come here."

Annot, still in the doorway, the ring clenched in her fist, shook her head.

Dugald smiled, a little sadly. "Can't you trust me?" he asked.

No, no, no, I thought, as Annot, biting her lip, walked back to him.

"May I see this ring, which is bringing us all to war again?"

I was close enough that I could leap up, grab it and run for the shadows of the back passage.

Chancellor Holden smiled as Annot offered the ring and the chain. Dugald weighed it on the palm of his hand, a fistful of gold with a smouldering ember of red. Holden held out his own hand, smiling in satisfaction.

"No," Dugald said, looking up. "Which of you is in command

of this—what do you call it? A patrol? A raiding party? Maybe an embassy?"

"Lord Hullmor is, sire," Annot said.

"Lord Hullmor." Dugald's gaze shifted between Romner and Hullmor, not certain who was who. "This ring belongs to Talverdin. Take it home."

Hullmor took a step forward. So did Chancellor Holden.

"You're mad!" he said. "Let them go and before we know it the land will be overrun with warlocks. They'll bespell the women and carry them off!"

Romner muttered something like, "Maynar help us, one awful orange-haired woman is enough."

Holden was nearly frothing at the mouth, sputtering in his rage. "They'll come in the night and murder us in our beds!"

"If we had wanted to murder you in your bed," Romner said, loudly this time, "you would have been dead several hours ago and none the wiser."

"They'll hunt us down like animals for sport! They're warlocks! They're evil! Look what they did to your mother!"

"My mother committed her own crimes," said Dugald. "No one forced her to do anything against her will. And she at least had the courage to act, even if it was unwisely. Better that than doing nothing, ever, while the world rots around you."

Holden was not listening.

"You're not fit to rule Dunmorra. Your father was an idealistic fool, wanting peace with the warlocks, but even King Burrage saw reason in the end. You, you're worse. You've been polluted by that creature you call brother. If they knew, your barons would depose you and give the crown to someone better deserving of rule. You betray humanity!"

Holden rushed at Dugald then, his hands raised. I did not see what he held, whether it was a knife or dagger or just clawing fingers. There was confusion as both Nightwalkers and soldiers grabbed weapons again, some to prevent the chancellor, others, perhaps, to protect him, and still others thinking the warlocks meant harm to the king. All I saw was Holden—the man who had burned my father alive, who had nearly burned me, the man whom Annot believed was her mother's murderer and who intended to kill every living Nightwalker in Talverdin—rushing to attack my brother.

A rage boiled up in me the like of which I had never felt, an upwelling force like fire bursting from smouldering coals. My vision went red and hazy, and the heat in my blood, my heart, roared from my hands into a sheet of scarlet flame.

The fire enveloped the chancellor just as he reached Dugald. Holden gave one long shrill scream of horror and collapsed. I screamed or shouted in my own horror and somehow pulled the snapping snarling flames back into the palms of my hands.

Annot flew to me and grabbed me. "Are you all right?" she demanded, shaking me till my teeth rattled.

Holden moaned. Dugald, very pale, looked down at him. "He's not hurt," he said, kicking away the long, slender-bladed knife that lay by the chancellor's twitching fist. "And neither am I, thanks to my brother." He offered me a hand up from where I still crouched on the floor.

"I think you frightened him," he said. "You certainly frightened me." He gave me a slightly shaken smile. "Maurey—thank you."

I shook my head. I could find no words to protest my ignorance of what I had done.

"I don't believe it." That was Romner. "No one has done anything like that in generations. How does an ignorant half-breed end up with that sort of power?" But the look of relief he gave me took the venom from his words.

Maybe most of the venom had always been in my own ears.

"Lord Hullmor." Dugald held out the ring, swinging on its chain. "Take this, before anything else happens."

Hullmor walked up to the king and ducked his head. Dugald dropped the chain over it.

"Tell your king—"

"Queen, Your Grace," Hullmor corrected.

"Tell her Dunmorra has no intention of invading Talverdin."

"Is that the truth?"

"Yes," said Dugald, "I swear it, by the shades of my ancestors: I am king of Dunmorra, and I say I will not permit my nation to begin a war on yours. And may the Seven damn my shade to eternal wandering if I break this oath."

Hullmor, with Aljess and Jessmyn hovering dangerously at his side, both with naked blades again, nodded. "I will take your words to my queen," he said formally, giving Dugald a brief bow, "if you will grant us safe passage back to the Westwood where we have left our horses and as far as Greyrock Town. All of us, should we all wish to go. And if you will guarantee the safety of the Baroness Oakhold and Prince Maurey, if they choose to remain in Dunmorra."

"No harm will come to my brother that I can prevent," Dugald said, "nor to the Baroness of Oakhold."

"It doesn't seem like you can prevent much," Jessmyn murmured. "Try harder in the future."

Dugald heard her and nodded as though he agreed.

Hullmor bowed again. "Are you coming, Maurey, Annot?" he asked in Talverdine. "We should leave while we can."

Dugald guessed what he must be saying.

"You can't leave yet," he said and held out a hand towards Aljess. Her sword was trembling in her grip, and her lips were pale. "Some of you are wounded. And—and this is a chance to begin repairing the damage that was done the last time Nightwalkers and Dunmorrans met. I give you my word of honor again, as a man and as a king, no harm will come to you."

"We can guess what that's worth," Romner said.

"Yes," Hullmor said, "perhaps we can." He touched the ring, hanging on its chain around his neck.

"Do *you* trust him, Maurey?" Jessmyn asked.

I hardly knew him.

"I want to," I said.

"We would accept your word, Your Grace," Hullmor said, "but I don't think you can speak for all your court, or your soldiers, or your city. Not yet, even if you can remove Holden from power in your court. Perhaps we can hope, here, to make a peace, but you need to begin it among your people first. They've listened to men like Holden for too long. My duty to my queen is to take the ring home before it falls into the hands of any others who want to destroy us."

"You're right." Dugald agreed only reluctantly, I thought. "But you'll at least wait until your wounds are seen to. The surgeon to my household is a good man. He won't—he won't mind tending warlocks."

"He'd better not," Romner muttered. He put an arm, very

cautiously, around Aljess' waist to support her and looked a little surprised when she did not try to move away.

The king waved a hand at one of his soldiers. "Send for physicians and surgeons to tend the wounded," he said, "*all* the wounded. Tell the royal surgeon he must care for the warlock lady himself. And take Holden to the dungeon. From this moment, he is neither my chancellor and chief councillor nor the chancellor of the university, but a prisoner, charged with the crime of—" Dugald hesitated, as if trying to decide. There were several to choose from. Treason. Attempted killing of his king.

"He poisoned my mother," Annot said, her face pale. "I think I can prove it, now."

Dugald nodded. "Charged with various grave crimes," he said.

"But you can't lock him up, Your Grace," Arvol whined. "He's been badly burned by that monster. He'll die."

"His clothes are singed," Romner said, and for once I sympathized with the disdain in his voice. "He can barely have felt that. Your brother merely fainted, like the coward he is. The prince was more merciful than the murderer deserved."

In truth I had no idea what I had done and no control over it. Mercy was not on my mind. I could as easily have incinerated Holden completely. Just then, I would not have cared if I had.

Romner knew this perfectly well.

"You understand," Dugald said, addressing his men-at-arms, "that these people are my guests. An embassy from the Queen of Talverdin. Sacred, as ambassadors are. Any harm done to them will be an act of treason against your king."

"Yes, sire," they said, in a ragged chorus. Some spoke quite firmly. Perhaps Dugald had impressed them by the way he stood up to Holden. Perhaps they had realized how close Holden had come to the unthinkable crime of killing their king. Perhaps that had shocked them into a willingness to try seeing things the king's way.

One of them even offered Aljess her captured sword back, in trade for his own.

✣ Chapter Seventeen ✣
Partings and Beginnings

Although Dugald asked them again to stay longer, at least to rest until the morrow, Lord Hullmor would not delay. He was quite right. Dugald had asserted his authority in the palace, but it was too great a risk to keep that ring, the key to Talverdin's defenses, within human reach. There would be others who believed as Holden and Arvol did, and most of the king's court now knew about the ring and its function, since it had been on display in its brazier of philosopher's fire most of the summer.

It would be difficult enough for him to have the court accept me as his brother.

"You can't stay here," Jessmyn said, speaking in Talverdine. "You won't be safe, Maurey."

"Your brother means well," Aljess added from where she sat stripped down to her linen shirt, while a nervous surgeon, who tended the king's own household, stitched the cut on her arm. A scowling Romner leaned over him, which may have been why he was nervous. Aljess clenched her teeth on a gasp of pain, and the man murmured something apologetic.

"He means well," Jessmyn said, taking up her sister's thought, "but what if he can't protect you?"

"I have to stay," I said, "at least for a little while, long enough to make them see that I'm—human too. We have to start somewhere. If I can't make these people, most of whom knew my mother, all of whom are supposed to be loyal to my brother—if I can't make them understand that I'm little different from them, what chance does a real embassy from my aunt the queen have?"

Annot agreed. "Let them get used to Maurey," she said. "Let them remember that a large number of them actually supported King Burrage's peace plans, not so very many years ago."

"Will you be safe?" Hullmor asked her. "Ancrena told me to tell you that you are welcome to return to Talverdin, to live among us, if your own people reject you."

"I think so," Annot said.

"You don't know that," Romner, of all people, objected. "Think again. Come back with us; don't stay here surrounded by murderers and poisoners."

"Holden is in the dungeon and isn't likely ever to come out. No, I have to stay. I have responsibilities to my own people up in Oakhold, although I do want to come to Talverdin again some day."

"You'll always be welcome," Hullmor said.

"But what about you, Maurey?" Jessmyn asked. "A month isn't a very long time. You hardly got to know your family before we had to leave."

"I know," I said, "but I have family here too. And Annot's right in all the reasons I should stay here for a time. I want to come back to Talverdin, but I think I could do some good by staying."

"Set a date," said Hullmor. "Tell us when you will come back. Then, if you don't, we'll know to come and get you. Just in case."

Romner snorted. "That won't do any good if he's burned and dead."

"Nobody is going to burn me," I said. "I trust my brother."

"Tell us when you'll come back," Hullmor said stubbornly, "so that I can tell the queen I didn't abandon you here."

"The spring," I said. "I'll come—home, in the spring."

That did not satisfy them, but it was the best I could do. I knew it was important, even if it risked my life, to stay in Dunmorra for a time, and to aid Dugald in convincing his people that warlocks were not the evil monsters so many of them believed.

Once Aljess and the wounded men-at-arms were tended to, Dugald sent for food and wine and we had a meal right there in the Hall of Judgement. He also sent for some of his other councillors and had a loud argument with them. They were shocked and disbelieving that Holden could have attempted to kill the king. Some of them wanted to believe it was warlock magic confusing the king's mind. But the men-at-arms were there to tell what they had seen, and Holden himself, conscious, his hair crisped and his skin reddened as if by sunburn, was down in the dungeons cursing and swearing and threatening to throttle the king and me with his bare hands, if we ever came within his reach. So the councillors were forced to accept the king's words. They were a little frightened, I think, of this new, firm-voiced Dugald. Having so suddenly found he could stand on his own two feet after all, he was doing so for all he was worth, knowing that if he seemed to waver, some other councillor or nobleman would decide to take Holden's place.

Annot and I went back to the forest with the others to say farewell and to get our horses and Blaze. The girls all cried on one another's shoulders at parting.

"You'd think someone had died," Romner said in disgust. He spent a long time scowling down his nose at me, telling me over and over how to take care of my Owlfoot and Annot's mare

Moonpearl and repeating that he thought it was a crime to leave good Talverdine horses in human hands.

"Yes, Romner," Annot said. "We know you'll miss us. Some people would just say so." And with a grin full of mischief she kissed him. His treacherous ears turned bright red.

Hullmor reminded me again that if I did not come to Talverdin in the spring, they would come to get me. The twins kissed me and kissed Annot. Hullmor clasped my hands and Romner thumped me on the shoulder with his fist, and then they were gone, the black-haired riders and the tall white horses slipping into the forest shadows. Blaze butted his head against Annot's hand and whimpered.

"It's all right, boy," she said, scratching around his ears. "We'll see them again."

We rode back to Cragroyal in thoughtful silence. I, at least, was regretting that in all the flurry of farewell embraces I hadn't managed to steal a kiss from Annot, but she leaned over as we approached the city and put her hand over mine on the reins.

"I'm glad you didn't go back with them, Maurey," she said, looking at Moonpearl's ears, not at me. "I thought you would have."

I didn't know what to say, but I turned my hand and clasped her fingers, before she pulled away.

Some of Dugald's own trusted knights were on duty at the city gate to be certain we were allowed in. Two of them rode on with us as escort.

The people in the streets turned in silence to stare at a Nightwalker and Nightwalker horses riding up to the palace in broad daylight, a sight that had not been seen in Cragroyal since my father came on that fateful embassy to King Burrage.

Even that was not the end of it. The Baroness of Oakhold was granted a royal pardon for her part in my escape that past spring. The king was not certain that she had really committed a crime, as I was no criminal, but "better safe than sorry," he said.

Chancellor Holden was tried for the crime of treason, for attacking his king. At the same time, he was tried for the murder of his cousin-by-marriage, Annot's mother. The alchemical tests Romner had told us of, which the alchemy masters of Chrysanthemum College carried out on the long slender braid of her mother's hair that Annot had worn over her heart through all our adventures, proved that the late Baroness had been poisoned with stibium. Annot's testimony, when she swore by the shades of her ancestors and the Seven Powers that she had seen Holden putting his "tonic" into her mother's wine, convinced the three magistrates and the jury of twelve barons and university masters, whom the king had appointed to judge both cases.

Holden was found guilty of murder and treason. He was sentenced to death by beheading. Annot and I attended the execution, not out of any vengeful desire to watch his dying, but because it would have been cowardice, of a sort, to have hidden away, when we were the agents of his downfall, the living representatives of those he had destroyed, the survivors of his crimes (though the burning of Prince Lishon had been no crime in the eyes of Dunmorran law). I wept afterwards. I don't know why. It was not for Holden, nor even for the parents I had never had a chance to know—but for a world, I think, where men like Holden could go to their deaths still believing that in killing people like me they had done what was right.

Master Arvol was likewise found guilty, not of murder, but of embezzlement of funds entrusted to him for Fowler College pupils and students. He lost his position, and all of his property was confiscated to make restitution to the poor scholars (including me) whose funds had been improperly used or taken outright. And Chancellor Holden's estate was all forfeit to the crown for his treason; Dugald granted much of it to Annot, as the blood-fine for her mother's murder. She had a plan, which many of the university masters, though not all, were loudly opposing, to found an eighth college and grammar school at Cragroyal University—for girls.

The last we heard, Master Arvol had gone south to Eswy, trying to find work as a humble clerk.

I did not dare try to do any more magic, not then. My anger could so easily have incinerated Holden; who knew what I might do next time? Once I was back in Talverdin, where I could study with my uncle the Consort and the other Makers, then, yes, I would learn all I could, explore my talents to the fullest. Don't think I didn't find it difficult to set it all aside, but I had learned discipline, learned to be quiet and unnoticed, through years in the Fowler College kitchens. It was dangerous enough to win trust for my people as a Nightwalker at Dugald's court, without having some horrible magical accident demonstrate what warlocks might be capable of. I could be patient. For a while. It was just as well I was so resolved, since when I did begin to study the arts of the Makers, my raw strength confounded them all, and the skill to control it proved slow in coming, dangerous to myself and those around me. But that was all in the future.

In Cragroyal I merely resumed my academic studies, dined several times a week with Dugald, and contented myself with that. I did not see much of Annot, who had gone north to Oakhold to tend to her baronial duties. This let her avoid the worst of the gossip at court. After all, it was a scandalous thing, a young woman traveling alone in the wilds with a young man, and a Nightwalker at that. No honest man would ever marry her now… Nightwalkers had more sensible ideas of what was and was not proper. Not that we had been improper, yet. Anyway, Annot wasn't one to care what other people thought.

At least she had no stern new guardian to condemn her past behavior. Dugald took her wardship upon himself, since she had not yet come of age, but he didn't interfere in the running of her baronry. He said she seemed to know what she was doing; if anything, he ought to have asked advice from her on ruling Dunmorra. But he did not seem to me to be doing too badly on his own. His court was a little wary of this new firm Dugald, who appointed a new council of more tolerant and liberal-minded barons, knights, Sisters of Mayn and university masters to advise him, in place of Holden's favorites.

It was, he said, a beginning.

On the day in spring when I planned to leave for Talverdin, Dugald and I walked in the long portrait gallery hung with pictures of his royal ancestors all the way back to King Hallow. We stopped under a portrait of our mother. She looked very young.

"I still have nightmares, you know," Dugald said abruptly.

"About what?" I asked.

"When I was a boy and Holden was my tutor. When—after my mother ran away. When they executed your father, Prince Lishon. Holden took me to watch. He held my head so I couldn't look away and called me weak when I tried."

I remembered how Dugald had repeated, *no more burnings*, there in the Hall of Judgement. I put my hand on his shoulder. He did not seem to need me to say anything more.

"I hope," he said awkwardly, "I mean—I never did apologize to you. I should have had the courage to stand up to Holden."

"You did, in the end," I said.

Dugald shrugged. "The end was nearly too late. Maurey—how can you forgive me?"

I thought about that. "You're my brother. And since then, you've shown you mean the Nightwalkers well. You're trying to change things."

A letter from him to Queen Ancrena was packed in Owlfoot's saddlebag. It proposed an exchange of ambassadors and suggested that in a year or two I might come back to Dunmorra myself as one of those ambassadors. If humans and Nightwalkers were ever going to live in peace, Dugald wrote, it was important that each side learned to see that those on the other were not so different from themselves. We had made a start on that, this winter. I had no close friends in his palace or in the university, but people did not cross to the other side of the room to avoid me, and nobody called me "Night-eyes," at least where the king or I would hear. Some of the masters even invited me for extra tutorials to help me catch up on all the years of study I had missed while I was a kitchenboy.

It was a beginning.

"I used to have to pretend I had a brother," Dugald said wistfully. He grinned. "Of course, my imaginary brother was older than me. He was the one who was going to be king and deal with Holden, and I would ride off and have adventures with Nightwalkers."

"Really?"

"Oh, yes. Though of course they were always the villains, and I was the hero, not the other way around." Dugald shrugged and went on before I could say I had never thought he was the villain. "Perhaps I'll be able to visit you in Talverdin some day."

"I'll come back from time to time." I did not sound as enthusiastic as I might have. Annot had not answered my last letter, asking if she would come down to Cragroyal before I left.

Dugald looked at me thoughtfully. "I wasn't supposed to tell you," he started to say, "but..."

A loud barking and a skittering of toenails on the polished floor interrupted him. Blaze hurtled through the doorway and down the long gallery, his plumy tail waving. I nearly fell as he bounded against me, paws on my shoulders to lick my face.

"Shades be thanked, you're still here," Annot said, laughing as she ran after him. She pushed the dog aside and flung her arms around me. For a moment, I was too startled to embrace her in return, but then...well, I had no intention of having to regret another missed chance.

Dugald coughed and turned his back. Annot finally moved away as well, although not very far; she kept hold of my hand.

"Hm," was all she said, but her mouth quirked into a smile and her eyes fairly glowed. "Did you miss me?"

I gave her a look. She grinned. "I'm glad I caught you. I was afraid we'd have to hunt you all through the Westwood."

"Through the Westwood?" I knew I was grinning like an idiot as well. "Are you coming with me?"

"Just for a visit," she said and laughed. "A visit for now, anyway. Just long enough to give the old cats something new to talk about. I do have duties here in Dunmorra. Good day, Your Grace!" She finally let go of my hand and gave Dugald a belated, Nightwalker-style bow. She was dressed in elegant Talverdine fashion too, in trousers and a long embroidered tunic, with a leather jerkin over it. And she wore a sword, with an easy grace that made me wish I had spent more time practising with Dugald and his armsmaster this winter myself. She was going to make me suffer when we dueled, I just knew it. "I told the king not to let you go till I got here, but I was afraid you might sneak off anyway. I had to find a steward I could trust to manage my lands while I'm gone. Cousin Holden's man made a terrible mess of things."

"Did you?" Dugald asked.

She dimpled at me. "Ask Maurey. A man named Harl and his wife. They're from near Erford."

"Harl Steward and Hanna?" I laughed. "I wish I'd known. I'd like to see them again."

"That's one way to make certain you come back to Dunmorra then," she said. "What's the matter with Blaze?"

We all looked. After his enthusiastic greeting to me, the big dog had bounded off, sniffing his way around the gallery. Now he was whimpering, pacing back and forth along a section of the wall.

Shadows there shivered, thickened and parted. Lanky body, long nose, sharp chin…ears like a pair of sails. No one can help their ears, I reminded myself.

"What in the name of Phaydos are *you* doing here?" I demanded.

"You sneak…!" Annot's voice trailed off. She looked at the king and back at the Nightwalker lord. "You idiot, Romner. That's just the sort of thing that makes people afraid of you all."

Dugald, who for one startled moment had laid his hand on his dagger, tucked his thumbs into his belt instead. "It's certainly not good manners," he said and gave me a sidelong look that was almost a snicker. "Who knows what you might see?"

"It's not good *sense*," I said.

Romner shrugged and bowed. "Forgive me, Your Grace." He bowed again, to Annot and me. "Your Highness, Baroness. I haven't been here long—though I have to say it was quite entertaining, and I'm sure Aljess will want to hear all about it. I arrived in Cragroyal a few hours ago and only came into the palace looking for Prince Maurey when I couldn't find him around the university."

"Why?" I demanded, feeling a bit embarrassed at being addressed as "Prince" and "Highness" in front of Annot. Romner was doing it to be annoying, I was certain, and yet I glanced sideways to see how she reacted.

She did not seem particularly impressed. Then again, an Annot who was impressed because someone was a prince would not be an Annot who rescued scullions from dungeons. And that was the Annot who impressed me. She noticed me watching her again and shook her head, smiling, as she elbowed me in the ribs. Ah yes, Romner still had something to say to me.

"I was sent to see if you needed help in coming back to Talverdin. We were expecting you earlier this spring, and certain people began to worry you might be—I'm sorry, Your Grace, because it's clear that isn't the case—detained." Romner stopped looking so stiff and and gave Annot what, from him, passed as a friendly grin. "And the others, who trusted the king at his word, were starting to worry the prince would get lost in the Westwood again and not make it to Talverdin in time."

"In time for what?" Annot asked.

"The wedding."

"Whose wedding?"

Romner looked down his nose at her. "Jessmyn's and Lord Hullmor's of course. Do you think I'd have come all this way to escort a couple of humans…" He looked at me. "…Or nearly humans, to Talverdin, if anyone else who knew their way around Cragroyal could be spared? It should be Aljess' task, but of course she was far too busy embroidering a dress." His lip curled. "Embroidery! She's worse at that than she is at magic."

I winked at Annot. "Are you wishing it was Aljess' wedding dress, Romner?"

Romner looked startled. "Still an idiot, I see," he said loftily. But his ears turned red. Dugald coughed. "Lord Romner, I can overlook your lack of manners this once, though creeping into my palace in the halfworld might be considered by others the action of a spy, at best."

Romner opened his mouth, no doubt to say something cutting, but the king interrupted, holding up his hand.

"I understand why you would do this. But please, in future, bear in mind that my brother's friends are welcome anytime." The king paused, watching Romner gape, swallow his retort and redden with true embarrassment. "My soldiers and court all know this. Warlocks are to be treated like any other visitors to Cragroyal." Dugald gave a wry smile and added, "At least I've ordered so. And—the more you *do* come to the gate, the less they'll fear you."

After a moment Romner laughed and bowed yet again. "Your Grace, I'm humbled and I apologize. Next time I shall come in by the gate and test their courtesy with my presence." Being Romner, he could not help adding, "If there is a next time."

"There will be," Dugald said firmly. "I expect there to be many more journeys between Talverdin and Cragroyal."

Also by K.V. Johansen

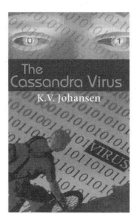

The Cassandra Virus

978-1-55143-497-1 $8.95 CDN • $7.95 US PB

"If there is one book that has shaped what I think a book should do and what literature should be," medieval scholar and award-winning author, K.V. Johansen says, "it is *The Lord of the Rings*." Like Tolkien, she is thorough in her research. Readers will be richly rewarded. Johansen lives in a bit of another world herself; she grows exotic trees indoors, from a Tasmanian blue gum that reached ten feet to several California redwoods. She shares her jungle home in Sackville, New Brunswick, with a large dog named Pippin and several enormous goldfish. Visit her website at www.pippin.ca.